BOYS WERE BOYS

ISBN: 979-8-218-62575-7
Cover design by: Yours truly.
Edited by: Marsha Worlock.
For inquiries, contact: whogivesashallot@gmail.com

For all the women who speak but are never heard, and for those with no voice at all.

TABLE OF CONTENTS

BOYS WERE BOYS

A novel by,
Lauren Hollander

Day Zero: Officer Flores – Boyle Heights, California

amila crosses her arms, watching as Patrick's thumb swipes across his phone screen in a familiar rhythm. Patrick finally seems to notice Camila staring, grinning up at her as he glances down at the screen one last time before sliding it into his back pocket.

"11:11, make a wi –," Patrick's voice cuts off abruptly as a crash sounds from outside, Camila's attention instinctively snapping towards the disturbance. Through the wide pane glass windows of the precinct, Camila notes a few civilians sprinting across the street in a panic, smoke beginning to billow and rise from just out of view.

Camila turns back to her partner, her body tensed and coiled, her hand going to the walkie clipped at her shoulder, ready to spring into action – but stops short, her brows furrowing in confusion at the empty space where Patrick had been standing only a second ago. Camila turns, her eyes frantically scanning the lobby for Patrick's tall, familiar frame.

They had been partnered for nearly a year now, and though Camila sometimes got a mildly unsettling vibe from Patrick – the way his eyes would follow a woman from time to time, lingering over her body with a predatory look that was always gone in a flash – he was, for the most part, a decent partner. At six foot three inches, he was hard to miss, broad shoulders and curly black hair often bobbing above the sea of cops crowding their morning meeting, visible even where he stood hiding toward the back, always slipping in at the last possible moment.

But Patrick is nowhere in sight, and there seems to be a shocked silence that saturates the open space. Camila's heart stutters as her eyes fall on Alice sitting at the duty desk, her face pale, jaw slack as she stares at the space in front of Camila where Patrick had been standing only a moment ago.

"What the fuck! Where did he go?" a distressed voice barks from behind her. Camila turns, feeling dizzy at the rush of adrenaline flooding her system, her brain unable to reconcile the events of the last few seconds and the almost haunted look on Alice's face.

Her eyes follow the voice to Officer Rennard, standing rigidly in front of the holding bench where a few spaces down a woman sits. The woman's wide-eyed expression mirrors Alice's, her hands clutching at her purse, knuckles white from tension as she stares at the empty seat in front of where Officer Rennard stands, his own head swiveling around the lobby as if in search of someone.

Their eyes meet for only a moment before muffled shouts from outside call Camila's attention back towards the street where she can now spot more cars piling up, the crowd around the crash increasing in volume.

It's as if the world was momentarily muted, only for everything to come crashing back in at once. Phones ring off the hook, their overlapping tones merging into a strange, discordant symphony. Beyond the halls, stretching away on either side of the reception area, Camila hears the rise and fall of raised voices, sharp and urgent.

She takes off without another thought, bursting through the precinct doors and out onto the street where a crowd has now gathered around a smoking car.

Camila pushes through the growing throng of spectators, her heart pounding as she fumbles with her walkie. She presses the button, her voice steady despite the panic she feels churning inside.

"Officer Flores to dispatch: we've got a car accident just outside the precinct. Requesting back-up and emergency services at First and St. Louis." The acrid scent of gasoline and smoke lingers in the air, mingling with the frantic murmuring of the crowd.

As she rushes forward, her eyes instinctively scan for that head of curly black hair. In the back of her mind, she reasons that maybe he saw the accident first – after all, he was facing that direction – and just got there faster. A small part of her protests at the thought, knowing she's the one with the sharper reflexes, always out of the car first, the one pushing through doors and chasing down suspects. It's not that Patrick is lazy, he just didn't seem to have the fire that she did. The fire that was required of her.

As a woman working for the Los Angeles Police Department, she simply had to be more. She had to be ten times – no, one *hundred* times better than the man beside her to gain recognition in this field. One small slip was all it took for her to fall. There were no locker room laughs and familiar slaps on the back for her. Every success was hard won, each mistake amplified.

Camila had decided she wanted to join the force right out of high school, carrying a chip on her shoulder as the only girl in a family of boys with something to prove.

But the seed had been planted long before that.

The Police Academy was a well-known landmark on Elysian Park Drive, as it was passed each time they visited Dodger Stadium. They used to go to the games as a family, and her brothers would make the same joke whenever they drove by the tall sandstone buildings, teasing that they weren't actually heading to watch baseball, but were dropping her off there instead. They said it like a playful threat, but to Camila it became a promise.

The LAPD required applicants to be twenty-one by the time they graduated from the academy, but Camila got to work right out of high school.

She knew the process would involve waiting, but between the testing, interviews, and counting down the days until she got the call that a spot had opened at the academy, Camila kept busy helping her father with his business and taking a few classes at East LA Community College.

Then, after years of jokes, her brothers finally took the winding road of Elysian Park Drive and dropped her at the police academy.

As the daughter of Mexican immigrants, she had learned early on that discrimination would always be a part of her and her family's experience in this country.

She could never forget that first beach trip the six of them took together. They piled into her father's truck, the bed cleared of its usual load of landscaping tools and instead packed with blankets, towels, snacks, beach toys, and the large umbrella her mother had picked up at a yard sale only a week earlier. Her parents worked tirelessly to provide for them, her mother pulling long shifts at a care home, while her father built a fairly successful landscaping business from the ground up. Camila could tell this trip was something special as they drove down the Pacific Coast Highway. Her parents' wide smiles were contagious.

The windows were rolled down, and the hot summer air whipped Camila's thick braids around her face, buckled in tightly between her brothers in the overcrowded back seat. The sound of their voices singing along loudly to *Baila Esta Cumbia* by Selena filled the air, dissolving as it mixed with the rush of wind and the hum of traffic.

They circled the streets for what felt like ages before finally securing a parking spot. With arms loaded, they made their way down to the crowded, hot sands of Santa Monica State Beach.

They managed to find a spot just big enough and began to get settled in, her father setting up the umbrella as her mother laid out the blanket and towels. At first, Camila was too focused on the array of treats to notice the dirty looks being shot in their direction from the family they had set up next to. As her mother pulled out a bag of chicharrónes and a container filled with brightly colored shrimp ceviche, her father's favorite, she heard a noise beside her and turned to find a mother and father with their young son, a disgusted look on the boy's face as his eyes swept over the spread her mother had laid out.

Camila immediately flushed at their stares, slightly embarrassed and confused by the emotion she saw in their eyes. It couldn't be disgust, she had thought. It was everything she loved to eat, it was their love language, and this boy and his parents were turning their noses up at it.

She tried to push away the heated glares of their neighbors, focusing instead on the laughter and joy of her three brothers as they called her into the water. They chased her through the waves, lifting her up over their shoulders before tossing her into the cool surf. Their hands were rough and playful, but they were always careful to never get too carried away.

When they returned to the blanket, their skin sticky with sand and saltwater, their mother scolded them playfully to wipe off before joining them for food.

"¡Mírate! ¡Sacúdete antes de sentarte!"

"Why don't you go back to your own damn country?" The father had said it under his breath, but just loud enough for Camila and her family to hear.

The heated stares from the family nearby were suddenly all too clear.

Camila was unexpectedly overcome with rage and not just for her parents, but for her culture, the country she was born in, as well as the one her parents had come from. They worked hard, paid their taxes – this was their country, too.

As she turned toward the family, angry words bubbling on her tongue and ready to spill over, her mother gently grabbed her arm and met her eyes.

No words were needed, Camila saw in her mother's expression a quiet plea to just let it go. In that moment, Camila wondered how often her parents had heard similar sentiments. How many times had they been shot dirty looks, words spat at them with hate in the street or while going about their daily lives? Had they gotten used to it? Learned to tune it out?

Even at nine years old, Camila understood that this country wouldn't be what it was without the Mexican immigrant workforce. She had never known people with a stronger work ethic – always ready to tackle the hardest jobs to provide for their loved ones.

On the side of the street, it was the white homeless man asking for handouts, while the Mexican man or woman on the other side asked for work. They sold oranges and flowers on the side of the road, tamales in parking lots, and stood outside Home Depot in the hot sun hoping to get a day job that could put food on their family's table.

Over the years she would have to listen to this hateful rhetoric, spewed by politicians and chanted in the streets, spat in faces by the most hateful and ignorant. "Get rid of them!" they'd say, while also demanding cheaper groceries, as if the two things were not intricately connected.

She knew then that it wasn't going to be easy for her. As she grew up, she noticed the way people looked at her brothers when they walked through a store or down the street together – those narrowed, suspicious glances. People would assume, without a second thought, that her honest, hard-working, and educated brothers were members of a gang, just by the way they looked, by the way they talked.

One time, she took her brothers to Target at the Eagle Rock Mall, and an employee followed them around the entire store. Her brothers didn't seem to notice, but each time she caught sight of the woman's pinched expression, the anger inside of her grew.

She thought that becoming a cop might make a difference. Maybe, if she wore the badge, she would be the one to get the call when things went south, instead of some power-hungry deputy itching for a reason to squeeze the trigger on the next minority who crossed their path.

She believed she could do it differently, that she could be the kind of officer who listened, who understood the weight of the job, who wouldn't fall into the same old patterns of fear and prejudice. But part of her still wondered if that ideal was just a dream. She saw the news. She knew what it was like for minorities, for women, in this country.

"Please stand back!" As Camila reaches the crowd, she forces the thoughts away, the looks of confusion on the faces in the lobby, blank spaces where people ought to be…

"Get back!" Camila forces authority into her tone as the crowd slowly parts, revealing a woman sitting on the curb. A few feet away is the scene of the accident, smoke billowing from the engine, the front of the car partially resting atop a downed street sign.

Behind the woman a man crouches, his hand resting on her shoulder, other hand gently applying pressure to her forehead with what looks like a stack of fast-food napkins. Beneath the brown wad, Camila can see a trickle of blood cutting across the woman's face, slightly dried where a few drops have fallen from her chin onto her peach-colored blouse, staining the fabric.

As soon as the man spots her, his eyes go wide, his attention snapping to her, eyes darting over her uniform, the badge pinned to her shirt and gun at her hip. Camila is familiar with the reaction, a response to her authority. She can understand how some people get drunk on this, how easily it would be to take advantage of the power that comes with simply slipping on the uniform. Camila understands it because she feels it herself every morning before she closes her locker door. That final look she always takes in the mirror. Her dark hair slicked into a tight bun, uniform clean and impeccably pressed.

"Officer." The man acknowledges her presence with a small nod before continuing. "I got her out of the car and have just been applying pressure to the wound on her head. It didn't look too deep but was bleeding a lot."

"Were you the driver?" The man pales slightly at the inquiry, his body going tense as he shakes his head vehemently.

"No, he's my boyfriend." A young woman steps up from the crowd, standing behind him in support. "We were behind them when the driver seemed to lose control. Suddenly the car just jerked off the road and went up on the curb and straight into the sign. He pulled her out of the car just as it started smoking." The woman looks nervous but proud as she recounts the story, looking down at her boyfriend with a small smile.

"And the driver?" Camila asks, scanning the crowd briefly.

"I don't know, by the tIme we got to the car he was gone."

"We didn't see him," the girlfriend says in confirmation.

Camila follows her gaze back to the man, who is watching her carefully in turn, as if awaiting her judgement. Camila nods her head in thanks and kneels down in front of the woman who looks dazed, blood already dried and caked along her hairline where the bundle of napkins are being held.

"We called 911 as soon as it happened," he murmurs from beside her. As if summoned by his words, Camila can hear the faint sound of sirens in the distance.

"I'm gunna need everyone to take another few steps back." Camila sighs in relief at Officer Rennard's voice but can't help feeling a slight pang of panic that there's an accident in front of a station and they are the only two officers on scene, and Patrick still nowhere in sight.

Camila turns back to the woman as the sirens increase in volume, only a few blocks away now.

"Ma'am, where is the driver?" Though the question is aimed at the injured woman, her eyes go again to the good Samaritan and his girlfriend, scanning the other bystanders more thoroughly, as if expecting to spot the driver still there among them.

"My–," the woman's voice comes out as a croak and Camila's attention shoots back to her, noting the now familiar expression on her face – eyes glazed over, staring at the smoking car and the empty driver's seat.

"Ma'am." Camila tries for gentle but can't help the panic that threatens to boil over, coming through clearly in the tone of her voice.

"Did the driver run off?" Camila tries, hoping to get something out of her before she's taken away, the ambulance now in view, rushing down the street towards them.

"My husband… he just–." The ambulance pulls up, and a man and woman jump out, springing into action. Camila stands up and sidesteps as the EMT moves into the woman's space and begins checking her vitals, the helpful stranger finally taking his hand off the wad of napkins and stepping back beside his girlfriend.

"Where did he go?" Camila asks again, the small bubble of panic growing in her chest every moment that passes in silence.

"What's going on?" The male EMT asks under his breath, his voice shaky. "Within the past few minutes there have been calls non-stop."

"What?" Camila turns to him, taking a deep, steadying breath as her vision tunnels slightly, going blurry around the edges. Camila can almost hear it now – a distant buzz, the rising sounds of discontent and dread swirling around her, like a busy backing track coming to life.

"Officer, I'm sorry I'm going to need you to step back. We need to get her to the hospital. She may have a concussion." The female EMT stands up, while her male counterpart only offers Camila a small shrug, his features tight as he shakes his head and loads the injured woman onto the stretcher.

Camila follows close behind, feeling a sense of urgency to get the answer, now only seconds before she's taken away.

Earning herself an annoyed look from the female EMT, Camila presses, "Please. It's important you tell us where the driver went," unable to help the pleading tone in her voice.

The woman finally meets her eyes as the stretcher is lifted into the back, her voice barely a whisper as the doors begin to close.

"He disappeared. Just…gone."

Camila stands frozen as the ambulance doors slam shut and it peels away, its siren fading while the words replay on a loop in her mind.

She scans the crowd for Officer Rennard, hoping he can answer the questions now flooding her mind. People begin to disperse, some looking faintly confused, some panicked, others staring fixatedly down at their phones.

Spotting a figure running toward the building, she pushes through the thinning throng, shouting, "Rennard!"

He stops at the door and turns, his eyes flashing with something – surprise or guilt, maybe fear – almost as if he'd forgotten she was there.

"What is going on?" she yells, no longer able to contain the panic that's been building within. Patrick, the missing driver, the look on Alice's face, the empty handcuffs swinging off the holding bench.

"I–," he stammers, looking at a loss for words, one hand gripping the door, the other raking through his sandy hair. Kenny, usually calm, careful, and sweet, now seems stricken – his customary composure shattered. There is a visible panic in his eyes, a frantic energy in the way his hands tremble as if he can't quite grasp what is happening around him.

"People are missing, Camila." The way he says her name causes her throat to go dry. Though friendly, he's never called her by her first name while on duty. His eyes seem to be searching hers for something, wild and fearful and unsure. After a moment he shakes his head.

"I don't know. I just don't fucking know." With that, he yanks the door open and disappears inside.

Camila sprints after him, her breath shallow and ragged, as if she hasn't been able to run a six-minute mile since she was fourteen.

Something in the sky grabs her attention and she freezes, only feet from the door.

Having lived in Los Angeles her whole life, Camila is no stranger to planes taking off and landing from LAX, always droning and humming loudly from above. But this one is low. Far too low. It's not landing; it's plummeting.

Straight toward the earth.

Day Zero:
Keira – Martinsville, Indiana

Keira knew the moment she saw her father's truck kicking up dust down the road in the middle of the workday that it could only be bad news. It was only two o'clock in the afternoon, and he wasn't due back for another few hours. Him arriving home at this time could only mean one thing – her father had been fired again.

Keira had gotten used to his constant job hopping at this point, even dropping out of high school and getting her GED just so that she could get a job of her own, her father demanding that it was time she start contributing financially after he'd gotten "laid off" three jobs ago.

At seventeen, she'd already been working for two years – sweeping up hair at the local salon, a hostess at the small Mexican restaurant in town, greeting folks as they entered the supercenter, answering the phone at her cousin's autobody shop. These days she worked as a waitress at the local diner. It didn't matter as long as she brought money home for her father.

She couldn't help but feel guilty every time she squirreled a few dollars away for herself, the small bundle of bills hidden beneath a loose floorboard in her closet a sort of painful comfort. She knew that she was still years from freedom, but it saddened her that it was a freedom her mother would never, or could never, share with her. She would sometimes dream that she could save enough for the both of them. That one day the two of them could leave her father and start a life somewhere new. Live out a life like one of those cute mother/daughter duos on television. Like the Gilmore Girls, they could live in a little house or apartment together and give each other dating advice, staying up late and painting their nails, watching rom-coms and sharing from one big bowl of popcorn nestled between them on their comfortable second-hand couch. Keira had put a lot of thought into this fantasy, one that she knew would never come to fruition.

Her mother, Anette, was born in Martinsville, had lived in this very house her whole life. Her father had built their family home with his own two hands, and when her parents had passed away it became hers. And since she was married, it became her husbands by extension.

They lived on a secluded property in the rural outskirts of Martinsville, Indiana, a town with a population of less than twelve thousand. The one or two times he had gotten his act together long enough to be a decent father, he would take them out to one of the few chain restaurants in town, only having two or three drinks instead of the usual four or five. But it had been so many years since he'd shown her any kind of true fatherly love that those celebrations seemed like distant memories, perhaps even an illusion.

The slam of his truck door echoes through the quiet, followed moments later by the heavy thud of his boots on the front steps and the bang of the front door swinging open. The louder his entrance, the angrier he was, and today, it sounds like he's come home with a thirst for blood.

Keira knows what happens next, they have this routine down pat. Sometimes it takes on different variations, but it's always pretty much the same. Cast in a play she never auditioned for; a role thrust upon her through fate. An unlucky draw of the cards.

Keira imagines he wasn't always like this. She can vaguely recall a time from her childhood when he took an interest in her life that wasn't tainted by immorality and perversion. But that was a long time ago. Now, his only interest in her would earn him a one-way ticket to Hell. Redemption was long out of reach. The moment he laid a hand on her mother; the moment he cornered Keira in her room late one night – those were the moments that sealed his fate. But at one point he must've been a boy, just a child.

Sometimes, in the depths of her despair, Keira would wonder who had turned the boy he once was into a monster. Was he born with this seed of evil, something that lay dormant yet ready to thrive? Maybe it was passed down to him or transferred onto him by another. Her mother had mentioned a few times that Keira's grandfather was a rotten man. So maybe it was in his blood. Or maybe each baby is born a clean slate, and it is us – as humans, as parents, as a society – who corrupt. Who take this precious ball of clay and shape it into a demon.

Keira isn't sure she believes in God anymore, she called out for him too many times with no response. But she definitely would like to believe that Satan is waiting for her father, ready to dole out an eternity of punishment. A room prepared in his honor, fitted with whips and chains.

Maybe it was Lucifer himself who whispered in her ear from time to time, eager to claim his new patron. His honeyed words would tell her how easy it might be to kill her father. To slip a bit of poison in his food or push him off the roof one of the dozen times he went up the teetering ladder to replace a shingle or clean the gutters, drunk and dulled senseless.

He was due an accident; Keira just wasn't sure she could be the one to tip the scales. He sure as hell deserved it, but why did it have to be her? She already carried such a massive load. Even worse, what if her mother hated her for it? What if she was caught? Could she live with her mother being left alone, unable to forgive her only daughter?

Keira knew she couldn't be responsible for causing that pain, so she continued to build layers, burying her flickering spark deeper and deeper, convincing herself that her mother didn't know what happened when he visited her at night. She told herself that her mother would do something if she knew. But the truth was, her mother was broken – an empty shell of the woman she once was. Keira had tried to tell her once, but before she could even get it all out her mother had broken down into tears, whispering, and desperate.

"Please, please, please." Keira didn't know what to say. Please what? But to her, it felt like, *"Please don't burden me with any more."* They were both carrying troubles for each other far beyond what they could bear.

Keira had heard the threats, whether blunt or vague, he made them clear to both of them: if either of them tried to meddle, turn him in, get him in trouble, or escape, he would kill the other. Keira knew in her heart that he would, and he would most likely get away with it too. Even though he was a drunk, he was known and respected around town. He knew everyone and they knew him. He'd gone to school with half the town's authority. Keira and her mother didn't have a chance.

There was only one time he'd almost been caught.

When Keira was fourteen, she had fainted in class. The school nurse knew immediately that something was wrong with her. She held her in the nurse's office for hours, question after question about her relationship history and her home life, all of which Keira did her best to avoid answering. Even without blatant threats, she knew that nothing good would come from her honesty. Even still, the nurse picked up on something, and the next thing she knew the school counselor and principal were involved. When her parents were called to pick her up, she was petrified. Her father lied through his teeth, putting on his charming and easy smile, her mother quietly confirming all of his lies while sending her that familiar look of pleading, begging her to stay silent.

The drive back home was charged, the punishment hanging in the air, thick and heavy. Her mother couldn't get up for five days after that.

Keira learned to hide the abuse better over the years.

At seventeen, Keira was grateful to have a full-time job, staying busy at the diner and hiding her small tips away with the tiniest glimmer of a hope that maybe someday an opening might come. A way for her to leave without feeling as if she would be signing her mother's death warrant in doing so.

It wasn't an easy thing accepting the fact that you were weak. But she knew she was. There was no hiding it. She knew there was more she could've done then occasionally step in front of her father's hand, temporarily relieving her mother of the sting of his slap. All she could do was keep quiet, tiptoe around him, taking the late-night shift at the diner whenever possible to avoid seeing him at all. Maybe there was a strength in simply surviving – but at what point was simply surviving no longer enough?

Keira feared her mother was broken, that there was no fight left in her. In the quietest, darkest moments of her own despair, she even wondered if she was too. What if she never left this place? Had her fate already been sealed? Keira couldn't afford to let herself spiral into those thoughts. Instead, she distracted herself by watching makeup tutorials online, researching cute apartments in Nashville, and curating a Pinterest board full of images that painted the life she wished she had – a life that, maybe, another version of her could live.

A glass shatters in the distance, followed by a familiar shrill cry. Keira pauses, takes a deep breath, and then quietly steps from her room, moving slowly down the stairs, each footstep heavy with the weight of what she knows comes next.

As soon as she steps around the corner of the stairs, she can hear him through the open kitchen door, cabinets banging in his wake, a glass bottle slammed down onto a table.

"Those fucking assholes think they can just get rid of me?" His voice, already slightly slurring around the edges, causes her stomach to turn.

Keira can't make out her mother response but recognizes the calming tone of her voice. The practiced placating cadence she takes on to try and calm him when his temper begins to take over. Keira cringes, knowing that when it's used at the wrong time, it can make things even worse. Keira can tell that this is one of those times.

At the sound of the slap and topple of a chair Keira rushes through the kitchen door. Her father's dead, red-rimmed eyes find her in an instant, and the breath leaves her lungs.

Keira could never forget the first time she'd seen her father hit her mother. It had shocked her to the core. Not just the way her mother's head whipped back, her hair falling from her loose bun to land in front of her face. How when she turned back there was already a blooming red mark spreading across her face, a tear in only one eye from the shock and sting. It was that her mother did nothing except look at Kiera, another silent stare that asked – *Please don't say anything, don't do anything.* Her mother had been broken far longer than Keira even knew; fragmented the first moment he raised his fist to her. The love and trust that she once had for him shattered into pieces, so intertwined with her own identity that she had lost sight of who she even was.

Was there any putting her back together again?

"Shouldn't you be out working? Or are you as useless as I always knew you were."

"That's rich coming from you." The words leave Keira's mouth before she has a chance to think of their consequences.

But the anger flared within her without warning. The indignation that he was the one always getting fired, her measly paycheck the only thing keeping food on their table at times. Keira ignores her mother's frightened gasp, her eyes refusing to leave his own.

"What did you say?" Her stomach curdles at the look on his face, the sick twist of his mouth. She realizes her dire mistake at once, her confidence gone in a flash.

He often preferred it when she talked back, loving having an excuse to be even rougher with her, to knock her down a few pegs anytime he thought she might need it. *His little spitfire* he'd say from time to time, pinning her hands above her head, her struggle against him only increasing the hungry and crazed look in his eyes.

Keira looks down, her breath coming fast, not daring to meet her mother's wide eyes from where she lay crumpled on the ground, the overturned chair beside her.

His eyes flash as his gaze rakes over her, as hot as coals. Keira follows his eyes, flushing when she realizes she forgot to change out of the classic, fifties-inspired dress she wears as her uniform. She had worked the early shift, having come home shortly before him, and not expecting him back for at least another few hours. If they were really lucky, some nights he wouldn't come home at all.

Keira knew he was having affairs, and she assumed her mother had known too. She probably didn't care, was maybe even relieved in anything or anyone that turned his attention from them.

Even though her work dress was far from suggestive, she had developed early, and it was often hard for her to hide the curves that came to her so naturally. The ones that her peers looked at with envy, the ones she would've happily traded away the first chance she got. A moment girls looked forward to had brought her to tears. She knew what it had meant. She had seen the lingering looks, the clear thoughts forming behind his dead and glassy eyes.

In a second, he's on her, his hand in her hair, fingers wrapped so tight around her ponytail that tears spring to her eyes at the sharp sting. He wrenches her neck back and Keira can smell the whiskey and cigarettes on his breath.

"Always the little slut. Going out like that in your tight dresses." Spittle hits her face and she flinches, the strain on her hair increasing. "I know the things you get up to when you're out there." Keira hears the sound of his belt buckle unfastening and her stomach drops, wanting to fight from his grip but afraid that in doing so she will only make it worse.

His movements are unsteady, and he stumbles forward, twisting her neck even further as the counter behind her stabs into her lower back. At the sound of his zipper, she can't hold back anymore, her animal instincts kicking in as she tries to squirm out of his grip. He's never done something like this in front of her mother, and the thought of it makes her sick as she unwittingly meets her mother's wide and fearful eyes.

"No, please. Stop." Keira murmurs, the tears now flowing freely down her face. Her father's only response is a grunt, a hoarse chuckle as he leers down at her, his hand moving out of view.

Out of the corner of her eye, her mother stands, a look of fierce determination on her face unlike anything Keira has ever seen. A moment of clarity after years of averting her gaze.

"Leave her alone!" Her voice is primal, commanding, and Keira is startled to see her father flinch at the sound. The brief distraction is enough for him to loosen his grip on her hair, allowing her to slip free from the space between his body and the counter. Seizing the opportunity, she moves quickly around the table to stand beside her mother.

For a moment they stare each other down, and Keira is fleetingly filled with pride, overwhelmed by her mother's strength. But in a second, it's gone. Her father's face transforms, the evil intent in his eyes sending a shiver down her spine.

"What the *fuck* do you think you're gunna do, huh?" He throws the table out of the way with one easy swipe, the contents spilling across the floor, salt and pepper shakers clattering, apples bouncing and rolling across the tiled surface. Keira and her mother jump back, instinctively reaching for each other.

"You're *weak*." He spits the words, hot like venom, taking another step forward as they take another step back, only feet from the kitchen door.

"You're *pathetic*." He kicks the downed chair out of his way, and her mother jerks back again. But Keira is taken aback when she feels her mother's hands suddenly pushing her toward the door, an unspoken signal to make a run for it.

Keira thinks that maybe this Is the end, that maybe this is the culmination of everything. Time to fight back or die trying. And in this moment, she is grateful that she saw even a glimpse of her mother's strength, putting her life on the line to protect her daughter, her body as her shield even when she knows the potential outcome. They'd been walking this precarious line for years, knowing it wasn't a question of if, but when, it would all unravel – and who would be the one to pay with their life.

His hand finds the space between his legs, gripping himself roughly, his face twisted into a leer as he speaks. "You women are only good for one thi–"

In a blink he is gone. There one second and gone the next. No crack of lightening, no shaking of the earth, not even a whisper of wind. Simply gone without a trace.

The two of them stand frozen, staring at the space he occupied only a second ago.

"What...?" The word escapes Keira as a gasp, and their eyes meet, exchanging a look, silently seeking confirmation from each other, proof that what just happened, really happened.

Keira looks around the room, showing clear evidence of her father's tirade – the overturned chair and table, the glass shattered on the floor near the sink, the bottle of Jack Daniels and the half full tumbler, the now-bruised apple resting in the shadow of the pantry.

Keira watches in shock as her mother takes a deep breath and abruptly straightens, moving across the kitchen and gracefully avoiding the glass on the floor. She picks up the half-full tumbler of whiskey on the counter, staring down at it for a moment before throwing it back in one swift movement. She places the tumbler in the sink and walks to the closet, taking out the broom, and begins sweeping up the glass on the floor.

After a moment of watching her wordlessly work, Keira joins in, helping to set the room right again. She pushes the table back into place, gathering the items that had fallen – fruit from the basket, papers and bills, napkins, and the salt and pepper shakers spilled across the floor – before finally picking up the tipped chair and sliding it back under the table.

Across the table Keira meets her mother's eyes, noting something in them she's never seen before. Right then, the speakers in the living room, tuned to public radio, begin to broadcast an emergency alert signal.

Day Zero:
Zarmina – Herat,
Afghanistan

W ake up. Zarmina."

Zarmina opens her eyes at the soft, familiar voice, squinting up at the faint sillhouette of Shahar above her, gently shaking her shoulder. The blanket that covers her bed is pulled back slightly, allowing the dim light from the room to creep into the dark space.

"What is it?" Zarmina sits up slowly, her back sore, joints aching far beyond her years as her eyes find the clock on the wall, 11:44pm.

"The men. They're gone. Disappeared." Her voice has a nervous edge to it, but Zarmina senses something else underneath, an eager excitement.

"Disappeared? Gone where?" Zarmina swings her legs over the edge of her bed, pushing aside the blanket that hangs over the top bunk's edge, serving as a small privacy curtain in a room she shares with twenty other women and girls, ranging in age from twelve to herself, the oldest at sixty-five.

"I don't know," Shahar whispers from beside her, her gaze darting back towards the cell door.

Zarmina stands slowly, her arm on her lower back as she straightens. Her eyes adjust, revealing the plain metal bunk beds pressed tightly against the perimeter of the small space. The cell is little more than a concrete block, but you'd never know it from the colorful sajjadas, the thin prayer mats repurposed as bedding mats, and the threadbare blankets that cover nearly every surface, the bodies on the floor a tapestry of rolling hills.

Zarmina moves across the sea of bodies, never once stepping on a stray finger or toe, a landscape well known to her now. The other occupants of the lower bunks are stirring slightly, shadowed faces peering from behind thin sheets as she makes her way, Shahar on her tail.

"Rahila was being *interrogated.*" Shahar spits the last word, the disdain clear in her voice.

"In the middle of the night? I told you –"

"I know. I didn't notice." In the dim light Zarmina can see the shame in Shahar's expression.

"Where is she?" Zarmina takes a deep breath, her eyes scanning the now moving figures in the room.

Rahila was one of the newest additions to their wing. She was only fourteen, still a child. She had been brought in for a crime that seemed more a misunderstanding than an offense – caught talking with a man who wasn't family. She insisted he was just a tailor, that she had only gone to run an errand for her sick mother, but no one believed her. These days it didn't matter.

Women, especially young ones like Rahila, were being thrown into prison at an alarming rate. The whispers among the older inmates were mixed, some claimed the system had become harsher, stricter on women for minor offenses, looking for any reason to lock them away. Others said that girls like Rahila were simply caught in a web much bigger than themselves, trapped by a regime that saw their innocence as something to exploit.

Unbelievably, Zarmina often thought that many of the women in prison were better off. Freedom was an illusion for women – whether confined by the physical walls of their cells, bedrooms, basements, or homes, or by the invisible borders of their country. Over the years, women had already been denied jobs, education, health care, free movement, forced to remain covered and unable to speak in public. Now, they'd even taken away their windows, claiming that any space occupied by women in a house must not have a view to the outdoors. A prison in its own right.

Zarmina was grateful that at least she got a few hours a day out in the sun, even if they were trapped behind those chipped and dusty corrugated walls she'd come to know so well.

Zarmina grew up in a different Afghanistan for women, but she sees now that it was just the fallacy of her own childhood. Her knowledge of the world so greatly impacted by the bubble in which her foundation was set. Zarmina was born in Kabul in the sixties – what turned out to be the midst of their Golden Era, and the beginning of the end.

The girls growing up in this new world would never have believed that women in Kabul used to wear their hair styled, hijab wrapped loose and fashionably around their heads or necks. Women went to law school, medical school, engaged in politics and could enjoy a slew of freshly granted and hard fought-for freedoms.

That bubble popped in 1979 when the Soviets arrived, and unrest in the capital caused many to flee. Zarmina's family was among them, moving east until eventually settling in Herat. But from there it never got easier, as the 90's ushered in civil wars. The foundation that growing up in Kabul had granted Zarmina quickly began to crumble.

The new regime didn't see woman as equal citizens, and the laws quickly reflected such.

Women were rendered invisible, yet crimes against them only continued to escalate. Men were granted impunity, free to treat their wives as they pleased, while it was the women who bore the punishment for any transgression. Their religion had been stolen and used against them; its interpretation twisted into a knife used to cut out the tongues and eyes and limbs of women.

The men who dared to protect their wives or daughters faced punishment just as severe. Her father, a doctor, had sworn an oath to heal the sick, regardless of gender. Yet under the regime's rule, a male doctor treating women openly was forbidden. Even so, when a desperate woman arrived at their door in the middle of the night, pleading for help, he couldn't turn her away. He made secret house calls while husbands were absent, fully aware of the risks he was taking with every step.

Zarmina remembers the night they came for her parents – the heavy knock on the door, the sound of her father's careful voice, the echoing footfall and shouts as they forced their way into her home.

The gunshot, how it seemed to pierce her own ears as it sank into her father's chest. The sound of his knees hitting the hard tile as he fell to the ground, the blood that pooled around him as her mother's frantic screams filled the air. She was next.

It was only the promise, or rather threat, of marriage from one of the men that spared Zarmina's own life. Though for years, she often wished they had turned the gun on her, too.

Zarmina feels no regret now for killing her husband. Imprisonment was a fair exchange for being free of him. In a Western country, they might have even called what she did self-defense. The small knife she'd begun keeping tucked away within the folds of her chadari slipped into his neck so easily while he slept.

Before the new regime took over, the prison was run by a firm, but fair, woman. Shortly after they had taken Herat, she disappeared. Overnight, the prison was run by men, and the ensuing conditions reflected such. The young women and girls were being pulled out for interrogations at night, brought back quiet and bruised and brimming with shame. Suicides among the woman at the prison were at an all-time high.

Zarmina couldn't help but try to protect the girls however she could.

Shahar points to the huddled figure slumped against the metal door and Zarmina starts, noticing for the first time that it's been left slightly ajar.

Her heart stutters as she rushes forward, her steps quiet and sure.

Before crouching down in front of Rahila, Zarmina can't help but peek outside, the hall uncharacteristically silent and devoid of the usual two or three guards who keep watch over the eight large cells on their block.

"What happened?" Zarmina finds herself sneaking continuous looks out towards the hall, expecting the men to rush in at any moment and seal them shut once again.

"They were bringing me back from interrogation." The word was used because the truth would bring far too much shame. "They got the door open and then suddenly they were gone. Just disappeared."

"Are you well?" Zarmina asks, clutching Rahila's small hands in her own. She meets Zarmina's eyes only for a moment before bowing her head slightly in response.

Zarmina hears murmuring behind her, noting the occupants of the room, all stirring beneath their piles of blankets, sitting up and looking to her and Shahar questioningly, eyes darting towards the open door with a mixture of emotions – confusion, fear, anticipation.

"Wait here," Zarmina says softly to Rahila, placing a gentle hand on her shoulder. Zarmina stands and turns, nodding to Shahar to follow.

She pushes at the door, pausing as it creaks loudly in the quiet. Zarmina waits for a moment before she takes a deep breath and steps slowly out into the hall.

It is eerily empty, and Zarmina catches sight of women's faces pressed against the thick metal bars of the small square windows in the cell doors.

"What is happening?" one woman whispers, her eyes following Zarmina's movements with a fearful focus.

Zarmina shakes her in head response, looking around the empty block. Faces continue to materialize between the bars as she and Shahar make their way past the overcrowded cells toward the imposing metal door standing at the end of the hall. Beyond that door is the yard outside, the one they're let out into for a few hours each day, the tall walls blocking their view of the city beyond.

Zarmina could scarcely remember what freedom looked like, having spent nearly twenty years tucked away behind these walls. But she didn't mind – there was little freedom to be found beyond them anyway. Every new girl who arrived only confirmed what Zarmina had now long understood: in this world, there was no place for women.

Zarmina hesitates, her hand hovering just above the chipped green paint of the heavy metal door. The viewing latch is closed, hiding whatever – or whoever – may lie beyond.

She looks back at Shahar, unsure that calling out or knocking is the best idea. What would the men do if they caught them outside of their cell, even if it was their mistake that allowed it?

Their God demanded that all burden be placed upon women.

Zarmina steels herself, leaning forward to press her ear to the hatch. Beyond the door, Zarmina can hear the low hum of frantic murmuring. She holds her breath, focusing on picking up any of the words being spoken just beyond, but only one sticks out in particular – disappeared.

The voices sound young and unsure, and Zarmina takes a chance and calls out gently.

"Hello?"

The voices cut off abruptly, followed by a hushed, worried whisper.

"Hello?" a voice responds, scared and unsure, not at all the confident bark of the men who prowl the grounds. Zarmina picks up another round of hushed arguments – one voice placating, the other concerned.

"What is happening?" Zarmina presses, the tone in their voices giving her the confidence to pry further.

"The men – the other men," the younger one responds, his voice now closer to the door.

"We shouldn't say anything. What if they come back?" The second voice sounds a little older, carrying the emerging depth of manhood.

"They're gone," the younger voice states, surprisingly steady even in the face of what his statement may mean.

"That can't be possible. People don't just disappear, brother!"

"Do not think Allah is unaware of what the wrongdoers do. He only delays them until a Day when eyes will stare in horror."

"*Karim!*" the older one hisses. "How can you say such words!"

The silence stretches, and Zarmina fears for a moment that they may have disappeared themselves.

Zarmina almost jumps back when a voice sounds from just behind the door, the older-sounding boy summoning an authoritative tone. "Please go back to bed. The men were called away for an emergency. Everything is fine."

Zarmina takes another chance, forcing calm into her voice despite her pounding heart. "We saw the guards disappear."

After a moment the latch swings open and Zarmina steps back, looking through the window at two youthful faces. The boys look to be brothers, but their expressions are nothing alike. The younger of the two, Karim, stares up into her eyes, a surprising fire in his expression, while the older one, taller but slouched over, only glances to her wearily, his eyes darting fearfully around the open yard. Both carry rifles, Karim's slung over his back, the other boy's gun gripped in his hands, though slack at his side.

Zarmina can't help but take a quick look around the open space behind them, catching distant shouts from beyond the tall walls that surround the prison. Zarmina has never been out in the yard at night, but it's suspiciously absent of men, her eyes finding the tower where she'd seen guards placed before, now completely abandoned.

"How many are gone?" Zarmina asks, meeting Karim's eyes, as the older one glances nervously between them. He looks unable to relax, worried the other guards might reappear at any moment.

"We've only been able to contact five."

"Total?"

"Yes."

Out of the thirty or so guards that prowled the women's prison, only five remained.

"What about the male prisoners?" Zarmina suddenly wonders, it can't have just been the guards…?

Zarmina turns to Shahar, who has been standing beside her, just out of view of the window, listening intently. Shahar seems to catch Zarmina's silent question, turning and making her way back down the hall.

"We got a call on the radio from one of the guards remaining there. They don't have a count yet, but it looks to be about half."

"You don't think they might've escaped?" Zarmina knows it's impossible. Hundreds, if not thousands gone in a blink. Disappeared.

Herat Prison was never designed to hold so many, but under the new regime, its cells quickly filled beyond capacity. Some inmates were admittedly criminals, but countless others were guilty of nothing more than existing outside of the regime's predetermined lines. It wasn't just women who were targeted; men who dared to challenge the regime were also dragged in, packed into suffocating spaces. The men's prison bore the scars of constant unrest in a different way than the women's did – riots and deaths, brutal and unconcealed, often making headlines.

"Maybe, but –," they look between each other, a silent conversation taking place before the older one finally straightens and speaks up.

"We saw a dozen men disappear before our eyes." His voice is steady, as if finally coming to terms with the reality.

Shahar appears a moment later, confirming with a single shake of her head what Zarmina already somehow knew – not one woman missing.

"So, what now?" Zarmina asks, her voice quiet but heavy with uncertainty. Who would ensure their meager rations arrived? Would they be left to languish in their cells, forgotten, until some new regime eventually took over?

They both look to her, and it hits her then how young they are. The smaller one can't be more than fourteen, already wearing the weight of the world around his shoulders in the form of the weapon clearly forced into his hands.

"What are you going to do with us then? Will you let us out?" Zarmina knows they don't have the answers, but she can't help but ask. A new kind of freedom suddenly feels possible, not just for her, but for every woman and child locked away in the cells behind her.

Rahila – for simply talking to a man who was not family.

Shahar – who resisted a forced marriage.

Noor – a young woman trying to get a higher education, hoping that she could help the sick women in her village, but instead was dragged here, tossed way and forgotten.

Bibi – for running away from an abusive husband.

And the countless women lost forever to the shame inflicted upon them by circumstance.

"But you are criminals, no?" the older one asks, watching her with genuine interest.

"Son, our only crime was being born a woman."

Day Six:
Patsy – Chicago, Illinois

"Patsy!"

Patsy jolts awake, her neck aching at the awkward angle where it had been resting against the passenger window.

"What?" she mumbles, rubbing the sleep from her eyes as she tries to orient herself amidst the long country road that stretches out before them.

Patsy always hated her name. At twenty-seven, it made her feel much older than she was. But her mother had adored Patsy Cline, and so that was her name, whether she liked it or not. Her mother never saw it as outdated, a relic of the past, now often relegated to farm animals or pets. Her girlfriend, on the other hand, never called her Patsy, often calling her "baby" or simply, "Pats."

She rubs her eyes, finally conscious enough to notice the frustrated and slightly fearful expression Heather is sending her way, the look making it very clear that she's been trying to get Patsy's attention for a while.

Patsy hadn't meant to fall asleep so soon after leaving the campsite, but the few drags off the joint she'd taken with her morning coffee in front of the fire had been a lethal, but necessary, combo.

The smoke had slipped from her lips in a wide, sleepy grin, merging with the heavy plumes rising from the campfire as her mind refused to confront the reality of heading home, instead shuffling back though her favorite moments over the past week. Their annual hiking trip had been a success, even quieter than usual as they microdosed and hiked their way through the remote corners of Mark Twain National Forest. They spent each night beneath the stars, the sound of the fire crackling, skin tight from rinsing in the cool water of Jacks Fork River and drying in the early summer air. She didn't think much of it as she pulled the roach from the netted cup holder of her camp chair and lit up, propping her feet on the warm rocks. All she had wanted in that moment was one more day of freedom.

"Guess this means I'm driving, then?" Heather joked in a teasing tone as she returned from the river, toothbrush and water bottle in hand, sweatpants hanging low on her lean hips.

"Pats? *Hello*?" Patsy didn't even realize her eyes had slid shut again. She sits up a little straighter, shooting Heather an apologetic glance.

"Sorry! Where are we? Are we still in Missouri?" Patsy looks around, searching for a sign or familiar landmark. Patsy finally recognizes the section of highway; one they've been travelling down every summer for the past three years as they make the journey home to Chicago. Patsy planned the trip for their one-year anniversary three years ago, and since has become a tradition.

Both of their jobs keep them chained to the digital world, so their yearly seven-day retreat – disconnected from service, screens, and the constant accompanying noise – has become a ritual they require. For a week, they car camped, moving from trailhead to trailhead, rinsing off in icy rivers and lakes, before curling up together beneath the stars – so much brighter and more vibrant than the ones hidden behind the smog from the porch of their Skokie home.

"Yeah, we haven't even passed the interstate." Something in Heather's voice tugs at a nervous thread in Patsy's chest, and she sits up, turning to observe Heather more clearly.

"What's going on?" Patsy questions, noting Heather's anxious look, her eyes darting down to the phone in her hand.

"I dunno, something just feels off. I turned on my phone and had, like, twenty missed calls from my mom alone, and tons of news alerts. Can you just look?"

Patsy immediately opens the glove compartment, pulling out her own phone to power up as she takes Heather's from her outstretched hand.

"And the radio," Heather says, fiddling anxiously with the knobs as soon as her hand is free. "I can't fucking pick anything up, it's like total static."

"Well, yeah, remember? It's broken?" Patsy gently reminds her. Only a few hours into their trip they had stopped for wood, and while loading the bundles into the roof box, Heather had accidentally nicked the little antenna and shark fin on top of the car.

It didn't seem like it mattered, they rarely listened to the radio anyhow. Patsy had simply pulled the antenna off and thrown it into the back of the car to get fixed at a later date.

"Oh yeah. *Fuck*." Heather takes a deep breath, as if the reminder slightly calms her.

"Maybe you should pull over, babe." Patsy tries to force composure into her voice, as her heart begins to pound furiously in her chest, her eyes scanning the nearly hundred notifications on her phone, Heather's own now totally forgotten in her lap.

"Ok." Heather's voice is weak, but Patsy is grateful she knows her well enough to trust her rather than panic. They see the outskirts of Bourbon, an interstate town with a population dancing around two hundred, and slow, passing by a church displaying a message in large block letters.

THE LORD HAS CALLED HIS PEOPLE HOME – MAY THEY BE FOREVER WITH HIM IN GLORY

The town is eerily quiet, which isn't uncommon for a place like this, but the other times they've passed through there were other cars, movement, people out and about. Instead, it's almost dead. Patsy can't even hear the usual drone of the busy interstate only a short distance ahead.

Heather must notice the same, as the car slows to a crawl, and Patsy notes curious faces peering out from behind curtains.

"Here?" Heather asks, pulling into the town's small tavern, a place they stopped once or twice before for a bathroom break, the last stop of civilization before getting lost in the wilderness.

Patsy nods absently, her mouth dry as she scrolls through the secure message boards on her phone, her brain struggling to make sense of the information in front of her. The words 'missing' and 'disappeared' flashing repeatedly before her eyes.

Patsy had always been good with numbers and computers; a natural talent she discovered early on in life. It was all thanks to her mother, who had found a flyer at the library for a summer camp and simply decided to sign her up. Maybe her mother had seen something in Patsy that was craving an outlet, her confusion about her own identity that ate her up, finally channeled into something else entirely.

Her mother had moved to Chicago from St. Louis when she was pregnant with Patsy, following a charming white man who promised her a home in the suburbs and a happy life. She was a nurse; he was a pharma salesman. Tale as old as time. He left when Patsy was still too young to have fully formed him in her head, just a shadow of a man who had taken from her the parts she loved about her mother most. Her mother's chocolate-colored smooth skin and wide smile, the rich melody in her voice, her curves and edges and femininity that were so clear they begged no question. To Patsy's displeasure, she took more after her father, light-skinned and flat-chested.

By the time Patsy was a teenager, she had taught herself the basics of coding and statistics, and for her first project, she used what she knew about her high school crush through social media – her interests, favorite books, movies, and music – and created a simple program that analyzed patterns. The software would then suggest topics Patsy could bring up, like books or music, that matched her crush's tastes, but with recommendations that were maybe even new enough to spark genuine conversation. It wasn't sophisticated by any means, but it was the first of many that Patsy would create in her life.

This was also around the time Patsy learned that just because a girl was nice to you, it didn't mean she liked you 'like that.'

It took years for her to find her place in the world, but she built it, piece by piece. And it all started with computers, with coding, with learning how to quantify with ones and zeros what she couldn't understand about people and the world.

By the end of high school Patsy was something of a prodigy. While trying to decide her next steps (her mother strongly encouraging college), she had stumbled upon a fortuitous announcement. A major media conglomerate was running a competition that sounded right up her alley. All she had to do was create a machine-learning model that could help them target and increase user interactivity. The prize? A cushy job as a data analyst and a nice stack of cash.

So now, Patsy worked during the day, finding patterns and analyzing trends in audience behavior. But it was at night that her skills were put into something far more rewarding. She'd been part of a hacktivist collective for years now, using her data mining expertise to uncover social and political corruption.

Over the past six years, Patsy had been a key player in several important takedowns, tracking down the hosts of websites with illegal content that led to over a hundred arrests. Heather was the only one who knew what Patsy was doing late at night in the converted basement of their suburban home.

Now, Patsy can't make sense of the information in front of her, only realizing after Heather snatches the phone out of her lap that they're stopped and parked, only one of a few other cars in the small lot outside the tavern.

A second later Patsy can hear the sound of a line ringing, a frantic voice answering on the other end.

"Oh, honey thank God you're ok!"

"What's going on mom?" Patsy watches Heather's expression carefully, her normally delicate features pinched in concern.

"Nobody knows, just men disappearing out of nowhere. Only men! Your uncle Jack and so many others just – *poof*! It's been chaos! I was so worried about you, that maybe you'd–." Heather cuts a look to Patsy, shame in her eyes, and Patsy reaches out on instinct, taking her hand in hers and squeezing in comfort, despite Patsy's own anxiety lashing in her chest.

"Mom, I'm fine. Patsy and I just got into service. We are stopping right now, but still a ways out of the city. I will call you when we get back."

"Turn on the news, and *please* call me when you're home. I'm so relieved you're ok."

Heather hangs up without another word, jerking her head toward the bar's entrance. Patsy wants to say something, to offer comfort, knowing the intent behind her mother's words and the painful reminder they produce.

Heather's relationship with her family had been fractured since she came out as a trans woman at eighteen, and even now, four years later, the wounds remain. The rare holidays spent with Heather's family always put her on edge, waiting for that familiar misstep – some old story from her past life, when she played sports or was called by a name she no longer recognized. It was as if they refused to see the woman she'd become – the woman she was always meant to be.

Patsy's own mother was a godsend, living only a fifteen-minute drive from their house; her mother's deep well of love and acceptance never ran dry.

Patsy notes the few missed calls from her own mother as well, but instead of returning her call, Patsy follows Heather's lead out of the car, shooting her a quick text.

Just got into service. WTF. Will call you soon.

Patsy's phone pings almost immediately with a response.

Glad you're safe. Be careful getting home and give Heather my love.

Her mom had always been this way. Calm and collected, an unsinkable ship on treacherous waters. Patsy briefly thought of her long-lost father, wondering if he was one of the now missing men. Patsy would never know.

She could've found him many times over by now, but Patsy had resigned herself to the fact that all that remained of him were the traces she saw in the mirror.

It was clear that something had happened in the few days since they'd gone off grid, and from the little snippets Patsy had managed to read 'major event' didn't even cover it. The world they left behind in Chicago only days ago would no longer be the same one they were returning to.

As they step through the doors, every head in the tavern turns in their direction. Fifteen pairs of wide, curious eyes tracking entry. Patsy and Heather watch them with wariness in return.

"Hi," is all Patsy can croak out, Heather's hand finding hers at the intensity of the stares. Patsy notes it's mostly women that fill the bar, only two or three men to a dozen or so women.

"We, uh – we just got back in service from a camping trip and…."

"You haven't heard?" An older woman sitting at the bar gazes at them with a shocked expression.

"No, we –."

"Turn up the TV," the same woman barks at the bartender, and an older man behind the bar reaches up toward the TV, remote in hand. The woman turns back to them and gestures them over, making space at the bar closest to the screen.

Heather and Patsy share a brief look before moving forward in unison, sitting down as the bartender wordlessly hands them two shots of whiskey. Patsy can't help but glance up at the clock on the wall – 9:20 am.

When they look to the woman sitting beside them in question, she gives them a nod, and lifts her own glass, throwing the warm brown liquid back before turning her attention to the TV where a news report has begun. The rest of the women stare with open curiosity, watching the two of them instead of the report now blaring on the TV, as if desperate to witness their reaction in real time.

> *Good evening, I'm Maria Gutierrez, stepping in for Matt Johnson, who, as you all know, vanished live on television less than a week ago.*
> *That day – now widely referred to online as 'The Snap,' a nod to a popular comic book reference – saw millions of men across America disappear without a trace. Each day, more missing persons reports flood in. Current estimates indicate nearly one hundred million American men are unaccounted for, with the numbers climbing into the billions around the world as global reports continue to arrive.*

Heather shifts closer to Patsy, her hand finding her knee as Patsy's own hand meets hers. The whiskey in her belly sits heavy, the words ringing in her ears, grappling to fully comprehend their meaning.

A live graphic shows numbers broken down by states and countries, accompanied by a slideshow of portraits. All of them are recognizable faces – famous billionaires, actors, politicians, and athletes – all among the missing.

In a few moments, President Davis will address the nation. Sworn in just hours after President Hart and many members of Congress disappeared during an open session, Davis inherits a nation in crisis, with the country just months away from an election. The opposing party's notorious presidential nominee and running mate are also among those disappeared. President Davis's first act in office was to declare a state of emergency and mobilize the remaining National Guard to assist with the fallout caused by the mass disappearances. This includes devastating incidents like the four plane crashes across the country, one of which occurred near LAX, claiming two hundred and fifty-three lives.
Officials are struggling to distinguish between those who disappeared as part of 'The Snap' and those who were casualties of the resulting chaos. However, one fact remains distressingly consistent: for those taken, no bodies remain. Experts warn it may take years to determine the full scope of this unprecedented event.

The report cuts off and Heather and Patsy can feel eyes on them once again, intently gauging their reaction. Patsy only has eyes for Heather, unsure of how to react, looking to Heather for clues.

All Patsy can feel is a sort of weight has been lifted. Instead of anxiety, she feels an odd sense of – peace. A brief thought crosses her mind, and she wonders absently if, for the first time, she can finally run at night with both of her headphones in at full volume.

Patsy wouldn't call herself a man-hater, more like a man-realist. She's seen too much on the dark web to not think of them as evil, though she will be the first to acknowledge there are many outliers. She's known many herself. But her job has forced her to see darker parts of the world.

Just then a familiar face takes the screen.

"Wow, and I didn't even have to vote for her," Heather mutters under her breath with a wry smile.

Patsy snorts a quiet laugh, and grips Heather's hand tighter under the bar.

Our country – our world – is in mourning. We grieve not only for the men who vanished so suddenly but also for the countless lives lost in the chaos that followed. Husbands, fathers, sons – each disappearance leaves an immeasurable void. Today, we grieve together as a nation and as well as a global community.

In this moment of shared sorrow, I can't help but find a glimmer of hope. For the first time in a long time, nations across the world are coming together, united in purpose. Scientists, physicists, biologists, intelligence analysts and experts from every corner of the globe, both men and women alike, are joining forces to better understand the circumstances of this harrowing event.

I want to express my deepest gratitude to the National Guard, first responders, emergency workers, and volunteers who have stepped up in this time of need. Your courage and dedication remind us all that, even in the face of tragedy, our strength endures.

Your government is working tirelessly to maintain essential services and aid, and ensure our communities remain supported. There are already plans underway to reopen schools and public institutions safely in the near future, and we are doing everything in our power to restore a sense of new normalcy.

To those who are struggling, to those in need of help: we stand with you. Together, we will face this challenge with resilience, determination, and hope for a brighter future.

Thank you, and may God bless the United States of America.

It's well after ten o'clock at night when Patsy pulls into their driveway, the familiar crunch of gravel beneath the tires the only sound breaking the eerie quiet of the night. They had stayed in the bar for another hour after the news segment ended. Patsy had refused to drink anymore; Heather, on the other hand, had opted for another shot. A beer and two additional shots later, the patrons had bid them farewell.

The women spent a good deal of time recounting everything that had happened over the past six days to Heather and Patsy. Patsy was still shocked that they could've missed so much, but that had been the whole point of their trip – escaping the weight of everyday reality.

Sitting at the bar, Patsy mentally thanked her mother for suggesting the park all those years ago, a place her own mother had visited a few times as a child, where they'd spent countless weekends in the past. But Patsy never imagined that, on one of their peaceful getaways, something so world changing would happen.

Patsy had noted at one point that it seemed a few helicopters had flown over the forest above, but they had thought nothing of it, totally lost in it all.

It was probably the only reason her mother had seemed so calm. She knew exactly where they would be, tucked away in that remote forest, far from any chaos. There were no downed planes in Mark Twain National Forest, no accidents, no real reason to worry. It was probably much safer there than in the city.

And really, who could really plan for something like the end of the world?

There had been no signs, no warnings – just men all across the world suddenly blinking out of existence. One moment they were there, the next, gone. Like the flicker of a candle, snuffed out without a sound.

The usual five-hour drive from the interstate had taken nearly eleven. Patsy hadn't even considered how many cars might've been abandoned in that moment, their drivers disappearing with a foot on the gas. Thankfully, it hadn't been during peak commuting hours. Most people were already at work, but there were still outliers on the road at that moment – truck drivers, cabs, delivery workers, and those with untraditional work hours.

Tow trucks and emergency vehicles had been working nonstop for days, clearing the roads and highways. Hospitals were packed and understaffed, but it seemed like it had only taken six days before the fire had burned down to embers. The evidence was all around them, but it wasn't what she would have imagined.

When Patsy thought of the apocalypse, she pictured nuclear fallout, a fast-spreading disease, or all-out war. But this was clean, simple, quick. The injuries didn't come in waves, just one big storm all at once. There were no riots, no chaos in the streets, nobody taking advantage of the loss of government control. Sure, there would be a slow-down in the economy and food chain, but there were also now one hundred million fewer mouths to feed and clothe and house in America. The power stayed on. The internet still worked. It wasn't the collapse they'd seen portrayed in dystopian movies.

Patsy was relieved that the first priority had been clearing the roads. It was crucial for essential workers to be able to get to their jobs. Bus lines, though far fewer and emptier than usual, were still running for those essential workers. Everyone else had been told to stay home, with the majority of businesses temporarily closed.

The entire drive was slow and cautious, with a few tow trucks still at work clearing the roads. Stadiums and overflow lots had been co-opted, now filled with abandoned cars.

They had been stopped a few times on their way into and through the city by State Police or National Guard, diverted three or four times, asked general questions about where they were going, where they were coming from. Non-essential cars were no longer allowed on the roads, but after hearing their story, officials agreed it was extenuating and wild circumstances that found them there, and so they were sent on their way.

The second Patsy turns off the car and the garage door closes, they look at each other and release a collective sigh of relief.

"What now?" Heather asks, as inside the house, the phone begins to ring.

Patsy hops out of the car and runs inside, her shoes padding against the carpeted floor as she hurries down the hallway, snatching up the receiver of the old school phone that sits on the entry table. They never got rid of the connection, liking the thought of having a landline, the phone a large pair of glossy red lips. Heather even found a message machine at an estate sale, which is currently filled and blinking.

"Hello –" Patsy begins, slightly breathless, but is promptly cut off by an automated voice.

"This is a collect call from '*Patsy, please!*' an inmate at Putnamville Correctional Facility. Your call may be monitored and recorded. To accept this call, press one."

Patsy takes a deep breath, and presses one.

Day Fifteen: Zarmina – Herat, Afghanistan

Zarmina looks up from where she sits in the yard to see Shahar approaching, waving a newspaper in her hand, a wide smile stretched across her face.

"Zarmina, it's here!"

Shahar hands the paper over as she takes the seat beside her, looking at the women peacefully milling about the yard, some tucked together in conversation, others laughing. A sound Zarmina hadn't heard in so many years.

It had only taken a few hours for the news to begin to break globally. Mass disappearances, and only men. For the first time, women were the overwhelming majority.

Zarmina had sat up for hours that night talking with Karim and his older brother, Reza.

"What do you mean your only crime was being born a woman?" Reza had asked apprehensively, though a small amount of understanding shone in his eyes.

"Why is it you joined the regime?" Zarmina returned. The shift in the air was undeniable.

The brothers had looked at each other for a long moment, the weight of a heavy past stretching between them.

Once they began their story, it was like they couldn't stop, years of repression spilling out all at once.

They were originally from a small rural village, Sabol, and when the regime came through the town two years earlier, they had been pulled unwillingly into its cause.

Their father had taught them a different version of Islam, one that emphasized peace, tolerance, education and equality. When the suppression of their people, and indignities against women continued to increase, the new regime gaining more and more of a foothold in their country, their father's teachings only became more passionate.

Do not think Allah is unaware of what the wrongdoers do. He only delays them until a Day when eyes will stare in horror.

Their father had spoken those words on more than one occasion, and they also happened to be his last. He was dragged out into the town square, his body hung in front of a group of onlookers. The regime had promised money and food for those who would join, but they had understood that the offer was only a formality. The way the men had watched their sister, huddled behind their mother, was a threat in itself.

The brothers had joined, leaving their mother and sister in the care of their uncle, following the regime to Herat and eventually ending up at the prison.

They didn't believe in the teachings of the new order, but what other choice did they have? They stood by for months, watching the horrors of the prison, unable to intervene. Stuck in an existence with no way out.

Reza's eyes still darted around the yard, searching as if the disappeared men might return at any moment.

But as the alerts started to light up their phones, headlines spilling across the screens, the nervous tension in Reza's shoulders began to ease. Shahar stood faithfully by Zarmina's side, passing the messages down to the other women in the cells, hushed tones through the cold metal bars.

As the sun began to creep over the horizon, casting scattered shadows across the yard, Zarmina finally relented and returned to her cell. The boys didn't have the keys – couldn't have let them out even if they wanted to – but the bigger question loomed: what exactly did their future hold?

Zarmina barely slept a wink that night, the buzz of whispers filling the air, a world anew.

At eight am, only hours after Zarmina had shuffled back into her room, she was woken from a fitful sleep by a familiar voice calling for her from down the hall. She realized upon waking that the local mosque didn't call for fajr adhan. The women had missed their morning prayers for the first time.

By the time Zarmina had hastily dressed and made it down the hall, the door had begun to creak open, revealing Reza, Karim and the three other boys who had been left behind at the women's prison. Reza was the oldest at sixteen, Imran the youngest at thirteen.

The other boys all shared similar stories to Reza and Karim. Imran had been taken after his family was executed, forced to join the regime at only eleven years old; torn from his home and a weapon placed in his hands. They had tried their best to be men, to do what was expected of them, but it was clear they were just boys. Boys who all had mothers and sisters who they loved and respected.

And so, when Zarmina opened the door and Reza handed her the keys to the prison, the sudden weight of it all made her so dizzy that Shahar had to step up behind her, steadying her with a firm hand at her back.

When she had looked at the boys in question, they had just turned, beckoning her to follow. Zarmina handed the keys to Shahar and soon the women in their block crowded the small TV in the yard, where a news program played loudly.

It was chaos all across the world, not just Afghanistan.

It was as if nobody knew how to react, a shocked silence settling over the hundred or so women who crowded the small space, whispers fanning out like lapping waves as the news was passed backwards to those too far from the television to hear.

It wasn't just the words being spoken that had stunned the women into silence, but it was the sight of the streets outside Arg Palace, teeming with a predominantly female crowd. The scene was charged with overwhelming emotion – women pulling their niqab's down to reveal their faces, some screaming and cheering, others with tears streaming down their cheeks. For many, it seemed as though their prayers had finally been answered.

The man on television was reporting from the scene, looking eager but nervous, the emotional women pressing in on all sides. The dam had broken; it was as if everyone had been holding their breath for years, a collective pent-up scream now filling every airway.

Zarmina imagined there were still women who were in grieving, those missing their husbands, fathers and sons. Scared and confused, unsure of who would be their next captor.

Even beyond the prison walls, Zarmina could hear it now. The women's prison was located near the outskirts of the city, but the melodic tone of female voices rang in the distance, somehow still quieter than usual, absent the typical harsh bark of men. Those men who lurked around every corner, their dark eyes watching, waiting.

The regime had effectively disappeared overnight, the sun rising on a different Afghanistan that morning, one filled with potential far beyond anyone's wildest dreams. But it wasn't just the regime who disappeared; many, if not all of its followers, had vanished as well.

When the news segment ended, the boys again looked to her for guidance.

"I think we wait and see."

That day the women got back to their daily routine as if nothing had changed, but there was a shift in the air. The internet and power had gone out briefly, but services kicked back on shortly after with no explanation. The world somehow kept spinning.

Zarmina and Shahar sent the girls out like shepherds, spreading the news to the women packed away in the other blocks, releasing them cell by cell. The women picked up their chores again with ease, cooking and cleaning, silently processing the information in a mixture of hushed, excited and nervous whispers.

The television stayed on all day; the number of disappeared steadily increasing to the hundreds, thousands…millions. A small group of women huddled around to watch at any given time during the day, passing on the news as a new group came in to replace the last.

On the third day, a face Zarmina hadn't seen in years appeared on the morning news, and in that moment, she knew everything was truly changing.

Habiba Atta was a politician and human rights activist and had once been at the wheel of transformative change in Afghanistan. Her presidential campaign promised equal rights, education reform, and a path to democracy, rallying millions across the nation. But when the regime seized complete power of the country, the dream for a brighter future crumbled.

Anyone who had spoken of change that challenged the regime's interpretation of Islam was no longer safe. Educators, politicians, officials, lawyers, activists, journalists, and artists became the first targets. Many fled their homeland, carrying nothing but their voices and dreams and the hope that one day their country could be free.

In exile, Habiba became a force on the global stage, addressing world leaders and mobilizing support for all those left behind. Her speeches at the United Nations and articles in international newspapers painted vivid pictures of the suffering women endured under the regime.

She, and a handful of others, had been working tirelessly all these years to be the voices for the many who no longer had one. But their hands were tied. The crimes were recorded, aid extended where it could be, yet their country remained sealed off from the world.

Habiba had been living in Scandinavia for the past few years but found herself in Pakistan when the disappearances happened. Habiba had arrived in Islamabad only days before, working on an initiative to secure microloans for women-run businesses and was due to speak at a conference the following day.

When she was woken in the night, she could hardly believe the news. Under normal circumstances, saying that someone had simply disappeared just wouldn't cut it, but people had disappeared on live television, from cars, planes, right before people's eyes.

It seemed almost fortuitous that Habiba found herself so close to home, alongside three other women and a man who had also escaped Afghanistan, all influential figures in the realms of humanities and politics.

They had loaded up in a car together, and made their way across a border that only hours earlier they wouldn't have dared to cross.

Now her words carried the promise of a long-awaited change, a vision where Afghanistan could finally rise above its struggles. She outlined her efforts to collaborate with other countries, aiming to bring lasting peace and stability to the region.

With passion, she spoke about how Afghanistan no longer had to be seen as an underdeveloped country. She believed, fervently, that for the first time, Afghanistan had the opportunity to progress, to break free from the constraints of its past and embrace a brighter future.

Habiba spoke of freedom of press, of religion, of belief, of practice. That women were no longer relegated to the shadows, that they would be seen as equals.

"*She*, our beautiful country of Afghanistan, will finally see her time!"

Those final words brought tears to the eyes of every woman standing in the prison courtyard. Her voice seemed to howl throughout the whole city, playing through every radio and television simultaneously; a collective crack of the chain that had bound them in servitude for years.

She spoke from the front steps of the Arg Palace where even one week earlier she would have been shot before she even had a chance to open her mouth. A public execution to be made an example of.

Her strength became a beacon of inspiration, igniting a movement among women that flared to life in an instant; a country sitting on dry tinder, primed and ready to burn.

The news poured in after that, an avalanche of information from around the world that Zarmina hardly knew how to parse through.

Over the years, the regime had systematically choked out free speech, shutting down newspapers, blocking websites, and controlling access to both the internet and the news. But now, as if a dam had finally burst, information was flooding in by the bucketload.

It was chaos in the streets, but in a country where violent turmoil had been a daily occurrence, this was tame, different. At first, confusion and fear had rippled through the people, wondering if this was part of some large-scale attack. Yet, most had slept through the night, only to wake for fajr to empty beds where their husbands should have been.

Streets where men roamed armed with guns and twitching fingers, now free of threat.

Over the following week, Habiba had formed a provisional government and emergency council, pulling both men and women from law, politics, religion and infrastructure. Educated women who were so recently not allowed to speak in public, finally found their voices again. Elections were on the horizon. Habiba promised an open and fair democracy where every voice would be heard, but everyone understood that right now they needed a leader, someone to help build a lasting foundation on which they could grow a prosperous future.

Habiba addressed the crowded prisons, promising mass releases and forgiveness for crimes committed under an oppressive system, an opportunity for those who had been locked up to be a part of the new world they were building.

And so, five days after the men had disappeared, Zarmina opened the front gates, giving all women prisoners the opportunity to return home if they wished. The brothers, Reza and Karim, along with the other three boys, were among those who chose to leave that day. Some of the older women split off in different directions, each agreeing to take the boys who were alone under their wing. They poured out, dispersing across the city to their next destination.

Zarmina had somehow become the unofficial leader of their small, yet overcrowded, community. The night before the mass exodus, she had stayed up late with Shahar and the brothers, discussing more than just food rations and chore rotation. As Habiba pointed out, many of those in prison had been wrongly incarcerated, and it was time they were given the choice to return. Return to what – or to whom – nobody knew. But a new path had revealed itself, one that most had never dared to dream of.

She would never forget the sound of the final lock clicking open, the grating creak of the heavy doors as they swung wide. The eerie calm of the streets outside was almost dreamlike, the silence broken only by the shuffle of footsteps and nervous whispers. A few women stood scattered along the road, their eyes filled with curiosity and disbelief as they watched hundreds of women pour out of the prison, their faces a mixture of exhaustion and quiet victory.

Zarmina had wondered over the years what her country might be like if the regime fell. Those darks nights filled with poisonous thoughts, each time another girl had been tossed into the cells only to be dragged out again in the dead of the night. But in every scenario, there was more war, more tanks, gun shots, explosions, death and destruction – all for another group of power-hungry men to step in and begin the cycle all over again. But this wasn't that. This was something she couldn't have ever imagined. Those men no longer existed.

It was like freshly tilled soil. Pulled free of thorny roots and rocks and made fertile; renewed. Expectant and evolving. The promise of so much, too much, in the air.

Zarmina hadn't seen these streets in years, confined to these walls as the women outside were forced into their own. Now here they were again, eyes meeting across a dusty street.

Shahar had to shake Zarmina from her reverie, lost in a scene that she would've never dreamed possible. There was nobody to stop the women pouring out from the prison. No men standing with guns fixed, barking orders in cruel, commanding tones. There were only a few men in the street, who watched with weary interest.

Zarmina was relieved when Shahar stayed; she was the closest thing Zarmina had to family. There was nothing for Zarmina beyond these walls – no future she could imagine for herself. The girls in her cell had become her family, her mission. It was her purpose to protect and guide them, to keep them as safe as possible. Though with each passing day, Zarmina began to realize the threat she wanted to protect them from no longer existed.

The remaining women all shared similar stories – families torn apart, lives lost, and an apprehension of the uncertain world being rebuilt beyond the prison walls. With so much space now available, the women began to spread out, reclaiming a sense of dignity as the overcrowded cells finally returned to their intended capacity.

They had fallen into a comforting routine, watching the world play out around them.

Universities experienced an unprecedented surge, women flooded campuses, eager to learn and grow and step beyond the confines of their long-enforced societal prison.

They embraced the opportunity to study, to see their cities, to connect with their neighbors through a newfound lens of purpose and empowerment.

It had been barely two weeks, but the shift was palpable. With many men now unavailable for traditional roles, women could no longer be kept away from the workforce, instead essential to it. The demand for their skills in workplaces and industries grew urgent, and they rose to the challenge with remarkable speed and determination. Factories, offices, and classrooms once dominated by men were revitalized by the energy and ingenuity of women.

This was not just a period of adaptation – it was a revolution of self-discovery and societal redefinition. Women began to see themselves, and to be seen by others, as innovators, leaders, and contributors in ways that had previously been out of reach.

It seemed that many in the country had come to an agreement that this was an act of Allah. That He had passed judgment on those oppressors who sought to twist His word. Those men who remained had passed His test and were allowed to continue in their work. A line had been drawn firmly in the sand; men did dare not cross it.

Not a single woman had mysteriously disappeared, though a few were lost in the chaos that followed. It was similar to the rest of the world but far less catastrophic, as it had been nearly midnight in Afghanistan compared to midday in other parts of the world where the streets were busy and active.

"What do you think?" Zarmina looks at the paper in front of her. A picture of a group of women inside Arg Palace, with the headline – "Lost Prophets Returned."

"I think this is good." Zarmina looks up again across the yard where women are reading, stitching, laughing and talking.

"We won't be able to stay here forever," Shahar says, a surprising hint of sadness in her tone.

Zarmina can't help but smile at the irony of not wanting to leave the place she was forced into by circumstance.

"No," she offers, looking back down at the paper, her eyes scanning the words in the article.

It was bewildering how much progress had been made in so little time. For the first time in history, the entire world – every single country – had come together. It would take a while, but Zarmina felt excitement and hope for the future of her country and its wealth of new possibility.

Zarmina looks back down at the paper, her eyes catching another set of photos tucked into the corner, accompanied by the page number for the full article.

The pictures were from a rally in Herat just a few days earlier, close enough to the prison that Zarmina had heard the distant buzz of voices. A few of the women from the prison had even joined, including Shahar. The front gates, once opened all those days ago, had never been locked again.

The picture shows a massive crowd of women, laughing, crying, hugging, the woman who had stepped up as temporary governor stands at a podium, her arms open towards the crowd, a wide smile on her face.

Zarmina scans the pictures, her gaze catching on a woman wearing what looks like a vintage Kuchi dress, brightly colored and delicately embroidered, her long hair loose and wild in the wind. She stands out, vibrant and loud among the other women. The clothing of her people, lost to years of oppression, forced into black like the shadows they so desperately wanted the women of this country to become.

A memory of a photograph stirs – her mother, younger, standing among a similar group of women. Alive and wild and free. A fleeting glimpse of another time.

"But perhaps, Shahar, there's something, or someplace, even better for us."

Day Nineteen: Patsy – Chicago, Illinois

Patsy squeezes her eyes shut with a groan as the harsh overhead lights in the basement flicker to life, breaking the glow from the monitors, the only light in the room for the past however many hours. At this point, Patsy has lost track.

Nearly two weeks ago, she received a phone call from the last person she would've expected to hear from, but the first person she should have. Since then, she has been so immersed in her work, that if it weren't for Heather's constant check-ins, Patsy is convinced she might've perished.

"Baby!" Heather's feet sound down the stairs, worry and frustration in her voice. Patsy prepares for the impending onslaught, one she's heard many times before.

"You know sitting in the dark on your computers can cause eye strain! And you wonder why you get those bad headaches." Heather comes into view, eyebrows drawn, two Goose Island ales in hand.

"I know, I know," Patsy responds with a pout, accepting the beer and leaning up to meet her offered lips.

"How's it going?" Heather moves into place behind her, long fingers digging into Patsy's tight shoulders and neck.

"Fine," Patsy murmurs, her head rolling back, eyes sliding closed.

"Yeah?" The tone in Heather's voice causes Patsy to open her eyes, immediately closing them again with a groan. "*Ugh* these overhead lights though."

Heather laughs and turns on the lamp beside Patsy's desk, darting to the base of the stairs to flip the overhead switch.

"Better?" Heather bends down, placing a small kiss on Patsy's forehead.

"Much," Patsy answers with a satisfied smile. After a moment she adds, "I didn't mean to, you know."

It had been bright when Patsy started for the day, managing three hours of sleep on the couch before crawling back to her desk. Her workspace wasn't the typical converted basement one might imagine – dark and musty, creaking stairs and plush retro carpet. When they'd been looking for a house, Patsy had specifically searched for one that had a fresher basement, something with more than one ground level window. So instead of one tiny window, Patsy had four. The eastern facing panels still sat ground level but looked out to their sprawling yard and Heather's flower garden that had been framed perfectly around the window, adding to Patsy's view instead of blocking it.

"I know you didn't mean to, baby. We just gotta get you some time-activated lamps or something," Heather says with a fond smile. Her hands find Patsy's neck again, moving up to pull her long curly hair out of the band holding it on top of her head.

It was crucial for Patsy to have a well-equipped home office, given that her work extended far beyond the usual nine-to-five – and most of it done remotely. Before the world had ground to an abrupt halt, Patsy was only commuting downtown twice a month for check-ins and staff briefings. But just as important as finding a basement for Patsy, was a house with a studio space for Heather to work as well.

Patsy had met Heather at a small art walk on Halsted Street, and Patsy is convinced it was love at first sight. Among the bustle and colorful booths that lined the street, Heather was a vision in a knitted crop top and low-rise jeans, her long neck adorned with delicate chains and charms that swayed gently with each movement. Bangles jingled softly on her wrists, the sound carrying above the murmur of the crowd like a song meant for Patsy's ears alone. Her long blonde hair was braided back, strands catching the light and framing her high cheekbones. And then there was her smile, easy and shy, as if she didn't even realize the effect it had on people. To Patsy, it was mesmerizing.

It had always been easy with Heather, even when it was hard. Those first few dates, they spent entire nights just talking, peeling back layers and revealing the darkest parts of themselves for the other to see. They shared stories they hadn't told anyone else, trading vulnerable bits of themselves like it was the only currency that mattered. Both of them had spent so many years wrestling with their own identities, desperately seeking understanding and a place to belong. With Heather, it felt like they had finally found it in each other.

Trust had never come easily to Patsy, and she quickly discovered Heather felt the same. Heather often said, "Humans in general – but men especially."

Patsy had told Heather the truth about what she did after hours, a secret she hadn't even shared with her mother. It was a part of her life she had always kept hidden, and for good reason. What she did wasn't exactly legal, and if her name ever got out, it was more than just her job that would be at risk. The work she did for the hacktivist collective went far beyond the typical lines of activism – it wasn't just about raising awareness, it was about exposing corruption and holding those people in power accountable, no matter the cost.

Sometimes, that meant digging into places most people didn't even know, or want to know, existed, tracking down dark web servers hosting child pornography or sex trafficking rings – finding the people who thought they were untouchable. If the authorities ever caught wind of her involvement, it wasn't just a slap on the wrist. This was the kind of thing that could ruin lives, and Patsy was well aware of the risks. She didn't need the world knowing who she was or what she was doing. Even Heather, for all their closeness, could never truly understand the weight of it. But at least Heather was there, not asking too many questions, but sharing the load no less. Simply accepting Patsy for who she was – both the person who worked by day and the one who fought by night.

If either of them cared about or believed in the institution of marriage, they'd have done it by now.

Heather instead made them matching rings they both wore around their necks, simple and personal. In place of a wedding, they threw a massive housewarming party, their closest friends and family all coming together under one roof to celebrate the life they had already built.

These days, Patsy's mostly remote position was wholly remote, in fact, grinding to a halt completely.

The massive media conglomerate Patsy worked for had lost quite a few of its upper-level executives, including the CEO himself. A large portion of Hollywood's leading actors, directors, and producers had disappeared as well, making her job essentially obsolete, at least for the time being.

Patsy can't remember the last time she left the house, making it out of the basement for short bouts when Heather would drag her upstairs and force her to sleep a full eight hours in bed.

"You think this might be it?" Patsy opens her eyes, lost in Heather's ministrations on her neck and shoulders, fingers running through her thick hair.

"Hmm? Oh." Patsy follows Heather's gaze to the article typed out on the center screen before her. The monitor to the left displays what looks like a complex spreadsheet at first glance, but a closer look reveals color-coded columns and formulas running along the top. Each field on the screen filled with information, cells updating even as Heather watches. Meanwhile, the monitor on the right has a secure chat open, with messages from the others in the collective appearing in rapid succession.

"Fuck, I hope so." Patsy reaches up and stills Heather's hands, pulling her around the chair to face her. Heather leans back against the desk with a concerned frown, picking up her beer and taking a long sip.

It had taken only five days of Patsy doing what she does best to find a pattern in the disappeared that nobody else had.

Nobody had even thought to look.

Patsy refused to call it 'The Snap', as some had in the early days, as that implied a fleeting moment, something reversible – as if the millions of missing men would suddenly reappear years later. She couldn't bring herself to believe that. From the work she'd been immersed in over the past two weeks, it was painfully clear: the men who had disappeared were gone for good. Whatever had happened had been precise, deliberate, and absolute.

The panel of experts assembled by world leaders had made little progress, despite regularly announcing new 'breaking information' that ultimately explained nothing. Some claimed to have felt a shudder on that day, as though the air itself had shifted – like the charged scent before a storm. Others cited electromagnetic spikes, tectonic plate movements, or even planetary alignments. Patsy felt these theories were little more than distractions, designed to keep people complacent. The real focus, she believed, should remain on rebuilding the world – a task that, to her pleasant surprise, was progressing far better than she had anticipated.

"I heard the home phone ringing earlier, was that your brother again?"

"Yup." Patsy finally picks up her own beer, the thought of him weighing heavy in her chest.

It had been the first time he'd called her in over a year, despite an occasional letter that she couldn't bring herself to read. After their short call, with the promise to talk again soon, she had found the message machine full, his voice steadily becoming more and more panicked. She might not have taken the call if things had been different. But they'd just gotten back into service only to find the world in upheaval.

"How's he doing?"

"Okay. Better now. He's really hoping that all this might be a second chance for him."

Patsy would never forget the moment she got the call from their mother – her panicked voice, the choked sobs barely forming words on the other end of the line. Her stomach had dropped. Patsy knew immediately it had something to do with her baby brother.

Shortly after Patsy's father left, her mother met a nice man and remarried, and just a year later, Marcus had been born. Patsy remembers envying him in her earlier years, the way he looked so much more like their mother, how their familiarity was undeniable. But her mother was miraculous, the kind of mother who never let Patsy forget how much she was loved, how much she belonged.

Marcus was more than Patsy could've ever hoped for in a sibling. He was smart, motivated, funny and respectful. The whole package. Five years ago, her stepfather Charles passed away from lung cancer, and the three of them became closer than ever. When she listened to her mother's choked sobs on the other end of the line, it still felt like just yesterday that Patsy and Heather had waved goodbye to Marcus, his mom's old Honda packed to the brim for the four-hour drive to college.

That night, Heather had been the strong one, holding Patsy as she broke down, the grief nearly paralyzing. Heather had also shouldered her mother's confusion and grief, the three of them left grappling with the impossible truth of it all: how the sequence of events had somehow turned Patsy's perfect baby brother into a rapist.

Patsy didn't want to believe it – *couldn't* – but deep down, she felt she had to. Patsy knew better than anyone how men could be – she had seen the worst of them. She just couldn't reconcile the image of her sweet brother, the same one who could've gone to any college, but chose one only a few hours away so he could visit them whenever he wanted. The same brother who welcomed Heather into his life with open arms, who always made them feel safe and comfortable.

When Patsy first got the call, denial had been her first reaction. She remembered the frantic drive down to Bloomington, where her brother was in his first year at Indiana University, just starting to find his place in the world. It was unimaginable, but now it was their reality.

She could never shake the image of his stricken face, his adamant denials despite the supposed irrefutable proof. It was over before it even began, a plea deal signed, her brother behind bars.

If it hadn't been for Heather, she might have lost herself completely. Heather had been her anchor, pulling her back when the weight of it all threatened to drag her under. The things Patsy had witnessed over the years – the things she'd uncovered in her work – could twist a person, could pull them so deeply into the shadows that the very idea of light begins to feel like a cruel lie.

"Babe." Patsy starts as Heather's hands find her face, tilting her chin up to meet her gaze. "This right here is going to change everything."

Patsy feels the truth behind Heather's words. Hours of work compiling information that people need to know, even if it's not necessarily what they want to hear.

She had never seen the signs in her brother and spent years fighting the voice in her head that whispered maybe, just this once, to not trust the victim – especially when her entire identity had been built around doing just that. But when she opened the door after their long drive home and picked up the phone to hear his voice, she knew she couldn't avoid the conversation any longer.

"Pats thank fucking God you answered. You ok?"

So much had happened, it took her brain a moment to catch up.

"Patsy?"

"Yeah, uh, we are fine. Got back from our camp trip. No service."

"What the fuck? Wow, the timing on that. Yeah, mom mentioned it a while back but didn't realize it was *this* week. Didn't even think to ask her when we'd talked. Jesus." Patsy couldn't help but feel a twist in her gut knowing her mother had been talking to Marcus about her. Shame followed instantly. She should be happy he had their mother to lean on, especially since she had made herself completely unavailable to him for the better part of the past two years.

"Are you ok?" Patsy cleared her throat, trying to force the emotions down, feeling the exhaustion of it all hit her at once.

"Yes. It's fucking strange. Tons of prisoners gone – just, *poof!* At first, they thought it was some mass fucking breakout but, like, we saw it. Right before our eyes. It was just the middle of the day, people disappearing, guards even!"

Patsy didn't know what to say but was glad she didn't have to as Marcus went on, seemingly unable to stop himself. "You want to know the strangest part though, Pats?"

"Hmm?" Patsy felt dizzy, her brain, always so good at processing information, felt sluggish and overwhelmed.

"The sex offender wing, you know the one that I've been stuck in?"

Patsy didn't answer, her throat dry, knees weak.

"I'm the only one left."

"What?" Patsy felt Heather's hand on her back, turning her head slightly to catch Heather's concerned and questioning expression.

"Yeah. I mean, tons of prisoners went missing, but the sex offenders – all of them. Gone. Except me."

"I –." The sudden guilt was almost stifling. That first letter he sent, the only one she could bring herself to read. *"You know me, Pats."*

"We've been watching the news nonstop, like the guards don't care anymore, the ones left that is. We are all just waiting around to see what happens next. But the crazy thing is that there are some places saying that it was God. That he judged the guilty. That the ones who remained have, like, passed a test or something." He took a deep breath, seeming to collect himself.

Patsy closed her eyes, leaning back into Heather, her long arms wrapping around her.

"I didn't do it, Pats. I never would. Please. You gotta get me out of here." His voice was small, weak. That image of him sobbing in the police station flashed through her eyes. She had only arrived just in time to say goodbye. Forced to sit in an office and listen to two cops, who'd never once met Marcus, tell her who her brother was.

"I –," her voice caught, and long overdue tears filled her eyes. "I'm sorry." Sorry wouldn't even cut it. But it had been just the beginning.

Patsy fell into a fitful sleep that night, the information dancing around her head. It all had to mean something.

Patsy had slipped out of their bedroom in the middle of the night, carefully untangling Heather's limbs from her own. Pulling on an oversized hoodie, she crept downstairs, the quiet of the house and the world outside only amplifying her urgency. An idea had struck, and Patsy couldn't wait. She had to get to work. Obsession was just part of her nature – maybe even an unavoidable side effect of genius, tangled up with the threads of her own mental instability.

The first rule of patterns is to start small. If the pool is too big, narrow it down to something manageable. Focus on one small chunk and search for a likeness among the bunch. Once you think you've found it, test it on a larger sample size to see if it holds true. Keep expanding outward, refining and adjusting as needed, until the full picture starts to become clear.

Patsy found the missing from the prison easily, the lists of the disappeared had become a part of public record. She pulled their files, meticulously combing through each one, cross-referencing details and making lists upon lists until the patterns began to emerge. Once the pieces started to fall into place, she shifted her focus to another small pool: the local college. There, she repeated the process, digging into records, piecing together connections, and slowly building a clearer picture of the broader puzzle.

After creating four or five small sample pools, Patsy meticulously compared the data side by side. Patterns began to emerge, subtle at first, but then suddenly everything clicked into place, and the thread became unmistakably clear.

On day ten, Patsy submitted her work to the collective, and just like that, what had been her project alone became the work of hundreds. Within a week there was a private website with all the names of the disappeared in America. The members worked on the project day and night. Every time Patsy woke up and crawled back to her computer there was more. She knew the members were spread across the globe, each focusing more on the stats and data specific to their own country. She and the other American members worked day and night putting the final touches on the project. Hers would be the first domino to fall.

The website was finally ready, and it was Heather who persuaded Patsy to publish an article announcing its content and launch. The collective agreed, and once the article was live, they would use their vast channels to ensure it was shared far and wide, making it accessible to everyone.

Today was that day. There was no more delaying.

Wherever the disappeared men were, she only hoped that they somehow knew she'd figured them out. That the whole world would finally see them for who they really were.

Patsy stands and captures Heather's face, pressing her lips firmly, resolutely against hers. She pulls away after a long moment, smiling.

"You're right. This will change everything."

Taking one final deep breath, Patsy leans forward and, with one click, sends the information out into the world, then tugs Heather up the stairs without another glance back.

Day Twenty: Officer Flores - Boyle Heights, California

O ye, hermanita! Have you seen this?"

Camila looks up from her mug of coffee as Miguel slams his phone down in front of her with a loud thump. Camila shoots him an annoyed look, glancing down at the phone and back up to him.

"I'm not picking that thing up. Last time I got a fucking splinter," Camila mutters, looking over its cracked surface, a few pieces on the edge just begging to be lodged under one of her fingernails.

"¡No hables así!" Her mother shoots her a glare from the kitchen. "You know I don't like when you use such dirty language! Save it for the station, mija."

Camila kicks her brother under the table in response to the obnoxious grin he flashes her.

"Seriously, you're gunna wanna read this."

"Then send me the link, estúpido." Camila rests her head in her hands, exhausted and feeling like she hasn't slept in weeks.

Immediately following 'the snap,' as her brothers preferred to call it, the city was in absolute chaos.

It had taken nearly a week just to clear the roads of all the abandoned cars, the streets packed with vehicles left behind, their drivers vanishing into thin air.

Tow yards and parking lots were packed to the brim, their spaces overflowing. The country already had too many cars; now, it was just plain ridiculous.

The accident at LAX was another catastrophe all on its own. Emergency services had been flooded with calls, hardly managing to keep up. Every single response team was active, not allowing even a moment to process the full impact of the situation. There was no time to reflect on the massive loss until things started to die down. But as soon as it seemed like things were settling, a new wave of panic hit.

Missing. So many people were missing. The initial focus had been on the immediate disaster, but now the uncertainty of the disappeared was hanging over everyone. Families searching for loved ones with no answers in sight. The quiet had settled in, and with it, the unsettling question rose to the surface: where had everyone gone?

Camila couldn't have imagined a situation where declaring a state of emergency made her feel better, but in this case, it did. Troops were immediately mobilized following President Davis's swearing in. Countries rallied; communities came together. It was unprecedented.

It seemed like everyone knew someone who had disappeared. No one was more than two degrees away from one, or more, of the missing men – especially in Los Angeles, where suddenly the overcrowded streets were empty. It was like driving to Super A Foods on Christmas morning, except every single day. Camila lost her partner, Patrick, and in the days that followed, she discovered that a few acquaintances from high school, the police academy, and several other men she'd met throughout her life and exchanged socials with, were gone as well.

The station was understaffed. The whole of LAPD had lost nearly two thousand men, but aside from the constant flood of people still demanding answers, the crime rate had dropped to levels lower than ever before. There were still crimes, but they were small – petty thefts, accidents, drunk and disorderly conduct, a few altercations. No murders.

It was as if society had been reset.

But despite the lull in violent crime, people were grieving, the world was just a little off-kilter.

It wasn't just one country but every country, everywhere, was experiencing the same disorientation. Something was broken, and no one could quite figure out how to fix it.

Though it had seemed like things were moving in the right direction, there were still occasional reports of odd groups popping up around the world. Groups of men afraid for their life, a mix of panic and misguided unity, formed by men who feared this was an attack on their very existence.

It wasn't just about the physical disappearance of their gender, but the unsettling shift in how society viewed them. Some saw it as the beginning of a cultural purge, a sign that men were being erased, forgotten, or worse, eliminated. These men rallied under the banner of protection – of preserving what was left of their gender. But they were the minority, literally and figuratively. Most men simply stepped up along with the women. It was as if a mass majority of the remaining men finally understood that this is what it must have felt like for women all these years.

But not all agreed. Another faction of women arose, one that wasn't concerned with the survival of men as a group, but rather the need to protect the remaining ones – physically, emotionally, and socially. They worried about the lingering effect on masculinity itself, questioning what it would mean to live in a world without the same gender dynamics they had grown up with. But these were just whispers, side column articles, people who wrote on fringe blogs and in private chat rooms.

Camila's phone dings in her pocket as the twins burst through the doors into the kitchen. Hector and Gabriel weren't actual twins, but Irish twins, born nearly nine months apart. They looked so similar that people often thought they were identical twins, though most people who said that were white, so she didn't put too much stock in it.

"This shit is loco!" Hector says, gaze trained on his phone, Gabriel beside him, eyes wide and expectant as he looks at Camila, as if she should clearly know what he is talking about.

"They were all like molesters or some shit!" Gabriel says, pulling the chair from the table.

"Language!" The boys cringe in unison at the severe voice from the kitchen, moving to take their spots.

In moments like this, Camila can't help but feel a bit ridiculous being twenty-four and still living with her family. She had tried living away from home once but only lasted one month before she came crawling back to her familiar bed. She had taken a room in a house closer to the station, but it was just so empty and quiet, devoid of the constant buzz of life that filled her parent's home.

She missed the smell of her mother's cooking, her father's kisses when he'd join them at the table. How he'd smell of sweat and fresh cut grass and bougainvillea. How her brothers managed to fill any speck of silence with banter and laughter and conversation. Her older brother Miguel was twenty-five, and he'd never even attempted to move out. At some point Camila figured she'd take his cue, maybe they'd even find a house close by and she and her brothers could all move in together. It was more than some unhealthy attachment; Camila felt the need to protect them.

When Camila heard her brothers' and father's voices through the phone that day, her knees had buckled with the relief of it all. It had been so chaotic for hours that she hadn't even gotten around to worrying about them. But when her phone rang, her brother's face flashing across the screen, her breath caught, hand shaking as she answered the call. She was one of the lucky ones. Her family had come through unscathed.

"I told you! Read the article!" Miguel repeats with impatience.

Camila rolls her eyes but relents, her curiosity too strong. She pulls the phone from her pocket and clicks the link he sent, the three boys around the table now silently watching her every move.

The link takes her to a local news station that had reposted an article that went live at midnight. Overnight it had been picked up by every major news outlet.

A Global Purge of Sexual Predators – The Link
Between the Disappeared Men

Camila's heart skips a beat as her eyes dart over the article. There is no author listed, just an anonymous post on a website infamous for exposing secrets from the dark web. The group had been key players in taking down a ring of child predators a few years earlier, uncovering mountains of evidence that had been hidden on foreign servers.

"It's all over the news, people are going crazy, but like lots of people are coming forward and being like, yeah this person was a fuc –" Miguel shoots a quick look to the kitchen, lowering his voice as he continues. "Was a total creep or did this or that, like tons of people coming forward. They have a website up too where people can leave comments under people's names. You can even submit evidence and shit," the last word barely a whisper.

Camila didn't look up, her brother's voice fading into the background as her eyes scan the article, the lump in her throat growing with each passing word. The article laid out the methods behind their conclusion with an unnerving detachment – clinical, cold, and methodical. There was no trace of emotion, no pandering, no effort to soften the blow or apologize to those it might affect. It simply presented the facts: this is how we got here; do with this information what you will.

As her brother had mentioned, there was a link at the end of the article. They had compiled the names of every man who had disappeared in America, with other countries to follow shortly. Each name was tied to police reports, criminal convictions, and rap sheets. For those without a conviction, the outliers, they suggested these were likely part of the vast percentage of unreported crimes, cases silenced by fear, NDAs, or settlements. The article invited readers to search the names, and if they recognized one but had never reported it, they could submit evidence or comments anonymously. *You don't have to say your name if you don't feel comfortable,* the text read. The invitation lingered ominously: speak up if you want to or stay silent – it was up to you.

The major news outlet that republished the article followed up with a list of some of the most well-known names included. Among them were the former president and his infamous opposition, admired celebrities, chart-topping musicians, valued sports stars, and, almost without exception, every male billionaire. The revelation read like a who's who of power and influence, shattering the public's perception of these untouchable, almost God-like, figures. The sheer magnitude of it was dizzying; icons and leaders who had shaped culture and politics, been headline news, now exposed, accused, as being just the same as all the convicted on the list. People had already known these men were gone, but to classify them all as predators was massive.

Camila can't help but think of Patrick and his easy charm. Those brief moments when she'd seen his mask slip, back before Camila even had time to process what the face beneath revealed. Maybe she just wasn't great at recognizing the signs.

This thought brings a name to mind, one she hadn't thought of in years. One she'd forced herself to forget out of necessity, safety even. If not her own, then her brothers.

"I gotta get to work. Catch you guys later." Camila stands up and grabs her bag, heading for the front door even as her mother calls after her.

Forty men had disappeared from her station, including Patrick. Even though she had noticed something about him, something that made her feel slightly unsettled from time to time, he was a good partner. He definitely didn't have a conviction on record, otherwise he wouldn't have been hired.

That must mean that…. Camila shakes the thought from her mind, meeting her eyes in the mirror. She places the final pin in her bun, running her hands over her slicked back hair, and takes a steadying breath.

Her locker closes with a bang, and she looks around, studying the other women in the room. There seemed to be a tensed silence in the echoing space, the women talking in hushed tones to one another. It was clear she was not the only one who had read the article this morning.

If the article was true, then it was worse than anyone had dared to imagine. It was almost ironic how much attention had always been given to the idea of women wrongfully accusing men, as if that narrative outweighed the countless women who never came forward at all. We used to say that for every false accusation, there were thousands of silenced truths, buried under fear, shame, and systems set in place designed to protect the accused. Now, it seemed, the silence had broken, and the truth was louder than ever before.

The thought curdles in her stomach as she rushes to her desk, waving Kenny off with a polite smile as he lifts a mug of coffee in silent question.

After briefly glancing around the room, Camila pulls up the article again. The website is utilitarian, a simple searchable database with clickable links and an anonymous comment section.

Camila hovers over the website's search bar, thinking again of the name she hoped would never cross her mind again.

The thought of him fills her with shame, the memories rushing back as her fingers move slowly across the keyboard.

It was Camila's junior year in high school. Jason was sweet, a bit nerdy, an unassuming guy. They'd been in the Environmental & Conservation Club together for two years. When they'd go for beach clean-ups, and hikes in Griffith Park, she'd always find herself paired up with him, their seemingly mundane tasks filled with laughter and conversation. He was charming in an offhanded way, but Camila had never thought of him as anything more than what he was – a friend.

Right before summer break they had taken a weekend trip to Catalina Island. During the day she and Jason had walked along the beach, picking up trash and chatting about their summer plans. At the end of the day, when he casually mentioned that he had snuck a bottle of booze, and invited her to sneak away, Camila thought with an excited rush – why not? Her brothers were insanely protective with her, even the twins who were younger. But they weren't here to stop her, and Jason was just an innocent friend. In their years of friendship she'd never given him any indication otherwise.

What was the worst that could happen?

It didn't take long for her to find out.

They had snuck off after dark, giggling and passing a bottle of cotton candy vodka between them. Camila wondered where he'd gotten it, why he chose this sickly, sweet drink. Was it for her all along? Later, Camila would find herself absently wondering if his older sister, Tiffany, had gotten it for him, if she had known there was a girl going on the trip that he was interested in, if Jason had given Tiffany an impression of their relationship that was much different than how Camila saw it.

She remembers pushing him away in shock when his lips sloppily met hers, his tongue immediately trying to find purchase at the seam of her lips. When she opened her mouth to tell him to stop, he took it as a chance to slip his tongue in, wet and invasive, filling her mouth.

She had never been kissed before. She wasn't sure what it was supposed to feel like, but she knew it definitely wasn't this. At first, she had tried pushing him back gently, more concerned with how she could get him away without upsetting him. She didn't want to cause a scene; they went to the same school and talked to a lot of the same people. What if she did something that might make it awkward?

She laughed instead, something forced and slightly panicked, pushing harder this time at his chest. His mouth tasted like medicine, and she grimaced, this time finally mumbling "No" against his stiff lips and invasive tongue. But it didn't work. He kept going, his hands now groping under her shirt, stumbling around the cups of her sports bra, fumbling at the band of it as he tried to work his hand beneath it. It felt like his hands were everywhere, his strength somehow surprising her. He was tall and lean, but far from the bulky muscular frame of her brothers.

He pushed her back into the sand, and Camila could feel the cool press of it gliding against her back where he had pushed her shirt up, now trickling down into the band of her shorts.

When he crawled on top of her, Camila froze.

She had been pushing him off, murmuring "no" over and over again. Why hadn't he stopped? Did she have to be a bitch to get him to quit it? Did she have to hurt him? Destroy their friendship? If she yelled, then people would come. They would find them together, the near-empty bottle of booze beside them. She reasoned that she would only get into trouble. It couldn't be that bad, right? It's not like he was going to actually try and rape her – right? She was a virgin; he was a virgin. Everything she knew about him flashed through her mind as the thoughts went unanswered in her head. Yet she could only remain frozen, her hands still pressed against his chest, flexed against him, holding him back.

She experimentally pushed harder, but he only laughed, his head falling down to her neck, wet lips against her collarbone, holding her tighter as if they were playing some game. Like they were just two friends rough housing. Except she could feel him hard against her hip, his other hand travelling down her body to rest in between her legs.

She was wearing sleep shorts, the kind that were loose around the legs, leaving her far too exposed. She hadn't even thought of it when she'd slipped them on only an hour before, but now she was desperately wishing she'd put her sweatpants on instead.

Suddenly his fingers were prodding, trying to get around the thin layers of fabric, brushing against her. She panicked, one hand leaving his chest to grab his wrist, wrenching his exploring fingers away. The sand between them and around her made her itch and burn, her whole body buzzing with nerves, like she wanted to escape from her own skin, simply abandon her body there with him.

He chuckled again, as if the whole thing was a joke, as if they'd known each other intimately for years and he knew she was into this sort of thing. Like he actually thought this was something that she wanted.

He grunted and moved against her for what was only a few seconds but felt like an eternity. The whole time she held his struggling wrist as he tried to find his way back between her legs, finally stopping with a shudder and a groan that she'd hear in her nightmares for years to come.

He rolled off her so casually, the wet spot on his sweatpants peeling from her exposed stomach, sniggering awkwardly as if he'd done nothing wrong. So casual, in fact, that Camila wondered if he hadn't done anything wrong at all.

"Ok well. Goodnight." He leaned in and kissed Camila softly as she lay there frozen, her heart pounding in her chest. He stood, shooting her a small, shy smile as he snatched the mostly empty bottle from the sand and stumbled back to his tent.

That night, she didn't sleep. She walked straight into the ocean, hoping the salty water could rise away the shame.

Why was the shame hers to carry?

She replayed the scene over and over again in her head. How did they get there? He was a friend. She'd never given him any indication otherwise. Should she not have accepted his offer? She'd never drank without her brothers; they had made a rule if she was going to, they needed to be around. And frankly, Camila was a bit of a straightedge.

She'd just felt so free that day. The weather had been perfect, they'd spent hours enjoying each other's company and chatting about the future. It felt nice to have a friendship all to herself; as much as she loved her brothers, they were so tangled up in her whole life.

But as night turned into day, Camila knew that what he did was wrong. She said no, a few times in fact. She hadn't given him any indication she was into it. Why was it on her to have to be a bitch, to yell or hurt him to get him to stop.

When Jason saw her the next morning he smiled, a bit sheepish but not at all guilty. Not a trace of remorse. When he tried to sit next to her on the boat home she glared at him, setting her bag beside her before he had a chance. He looked confused, hurt even, something flashing through his eyes.

Camila couldn't believe it, didn't know how to comprehend it. It made her sick.

She didn't talk to him for a few weeks, thankful that summer had arrived, and she had no reason to see him. But he hadn't even reached out – she was the one to contact him first.

One night the anger and shame and confusion had been too much to contain. That past week she found herself reading articles online, her phone browser set to private. What was rape, consent, sexual assault? Every word she read confirmed what she already knew.

Camila had been scrolling through her phone when a picture of him came up on her feed. It was a quick snap of a girl hiking, taken from the back. Camila vaguely recognized the girl from school. That fire that had been simmering within her the past few weeks erupted, and before she knew it, she was sending him a message.

You sexually assaulted me. You realize that right?

He was online immediately, the three dots dancing as he typed.

What do you mean? At the beach?

Yes, at the fucking beach!

The dots danced for longer that time, her patience thinning with each rotation.

Wow. Camila, I'm so sorry. I didn't realize.

Her jaw dropped. How could he not fucking realize?

I said no! Like lots of times!

You're right. I just, I'm sorry but I didn't think you meant it. We were drinking and having a good time.

Did it seem like a good time when I told you no? When I tried to push you off of me over and over again? When I lay there completely still? Is that what you think it's supposed to be like?

He didn't respond for nearly twenty-four hours, and Camila hated that every time her phone vibrated with a notification, she'd pick it up, disappointed when it wasn't Jason. Did she really believe that there was some magical combination of words that would make what he did ok? That would wipe clean the memories of his sandy, sticky hands and wet mouth?

I'm so sorry. Don't worry, I won't bother you anymore.

Camila nearly burst with indignation at the words. She felt the need to push, to get him to admit that he had done something wrong, to spell it out for her instead of an *"I'm sorry"* that he hoped covered all the bases.

She decided right then she could never tell anyone. The times her brothers or parents inquired about her sour mood over the summer she simply deflected. She couldn't risk what might happen if her brothers found out. The risk of them becoming the men society already thought they were.

Jason didn't show up for his senior year. A few weeks after school started, Camila heard through the grapevine that his family had moved up north.

There was only one time she saw his face again, and it was maybe two years ago. A mutual acquaintance from high school she followed on social media had attended his wedding. Camila couldn't help the morbid curiosity as she clicked on his profile, scrolling through pictures of his wife and his work with kids in environmental programs. He was doing exactly what he had talked about doing that day on the beach. He seemed unaffected, totally fine. But was she?

The website in front of Camila loads and she once again glances around the office before typing his name in the search bar.

Camila pauses, steadying her breath as her mouse hovers over the magnifying glass icon.

The results load in an instant, and even though Camila knew in her gut his name would be on the list, she can't stop the pit from forming in her stomach at the validity this brings to the article's claim.

Next to his name, there's another link, and despite her beating heart, the slight buzzing in her ears, Camila follows it.

A cold shiver runs down her spine as she reads: *Arrested for sexual assault, no conviction.*

Only two years after what had happened with her, he had found another victim.

Day Twenty-One: Nari – Cambridge, United Kingdom

Nari wakes in a cold sweat, dreaming of his eyes, his smile, the warmth of his gaze. It's always the love you never expect that sweeps you up in the most surprising ways. The love of her life, gone in an instant.

At night, when she closes her eyes, the dreams of him feel so real that Nari wakes up these days with an ache deep in her chest, the pain and loneliness returning to her with full force. Each morning, as her eyes flutter open, reality crashes back in, and the events of his disappearance replay before her, unwelcome and unbidden.

That fateful Wednesday night, Nari and Edward had been in the kitchen making dinner, as they had many times before. The kitchen was warm and steamy, filled with the scents of garlic and sesame oil. Edward had brought ingredients back for dinner from Seoul Plaza across town – a thoughtful gesture he often did for her whenever he sensed Nari was feeling especially homesick, or when Edward simply wanted to do something sweet for her. It was just one of the many little things he did to make Nari feel loved.

Nari hadn't been home to Seoul in nearly two years, ever since she left for Cambridge. She always made excuses, saying she was too busy, that the school load was too big, or that she and Edward had made other plans for the break. But deep down, Nari didn't want to go back. She didn't want that life anymore.

Seoul was a modern city with traditional expectations. Her parents were upper-middle class and had encouraged her to go out into the world for an education. But at the end of the day, the most important thing to them was her getting married, starting a family and settling down. It was kind of ironic how they encouraged her to study something that she was passionate about, knowing full well it wouldn't be what she spent her life focusing on. They thought that college for her would be some amusing experience. Yes, she would learn, but she would get a taste of the Western world and its experiences and realize all too quickly that home was where she was meant to be.

But instead, the opposite had happened, just as Nari knew it would.

She found freedom in Cambridge, a city with distinct character and history. She lost herself in the picturesque streets and beautiful architecture, new paths unravelling before her with every new face and experience. She hadn't told her parents that she planned on staying, but the ring on her finger had been proof that England would soon be her permanent home too.

Edward was a romantic in a way that Nari had only read about in books or seen in movies. The day he'd slipped the ring on her finger, they'd shared a bottle of prosecco, spread out on a blanket on Jesus Green, the River Cam glistening in the distance. When he pulled the small velvet box from his pocket, Nari couldn't believe her eyes, even as the small hinge creaked open, revealing a halo of diamonds around an oval sapphire.

"When we graduate and get jobs, we can get properly engaged. For now, it's a promise. A symbol."

Only a week later, the night of his disappearance, he came home after class with thick slices of pork belly, pickled veggies, kimchi, doenjang and a plethora of fresh vegetables to make her favorite dish from home, samgyeopsal.

They had been together for only ten months, but it felt like years. He always showed an interest in her life, her family, her culture. The first time he'd come to her rooms with bags packed to the brim with her favorite Korean snacks and treats, she knew it had to be true love.

"So, what's the special occasion?" Nari asked as he pulled away. He had leaned in for a slow, sweet kiss, wrapping his arms around her and pulling her close.

Nari smiled up at him, leaning into his broad chest and breathing in the scent of him. She loved how he smelled, how his scent would linger on her bedsheets and clothes long after he'd left. Shampoo and sweat and reagents from working in the lab all day. Edward was studying pharmacology, wanting to work in the laboratory side instead of the corporate offices of his father's pharmaceutical empire.

"You. You're the special occasion." Nari closed her eyes, once again tipping her head up to meet his lips when suddenly the heat of him was replaced with the sound of glass shattering as the bottle he held in his hand fell to the floor.

At a sharp knock on the front door, Nari jerks upright from her bed, the reality flooding back to her as she takes in her dark and dirty apartment, Edward's crumpled sweater beside her, no longer smelling of him. Nari grabs her phone to check the time, her eyes immediately finding the string of notifications that fill her screen with concerned texts from her mother.

Nari's parents – her mother in particular – had been hounding her to return home. But it had only been three weeks since the incident, and the airline industry was still in recovery. Flights picked up again shortly after, but with far less frequency. But more than anything, she was in mourning. Nari feared that if she left this place, she'd never return. And it wasn't just Cambridge and her friends she would be leaving behind, but Edward's memory as well, returning to a place that never knew of him – of them. Cambridge had become a map of their love story, each landmark a portal to an earlier time. Each time she walked by Harvey's it was like she was back there sitting beside him, his hand warm on her lower back as they shared bites of a warm egg tart...

"Nari!" Nari slips her feet into her slippers and shuffles from her room as a voice calls outside her door.

"Hello?" Nari peeks through the eyehole, knowing full well who is standing outside her door, immediately spotting her best friend's bright red lips. Sighing, she takes a deep breath before opening the door.

"Did you see this?" Mercy asks, foregoing greeting, holding her phone out as Nari's eyes adjust to the bright light of the screen.

Frowning Nari reaches forward, taking the phone from her hand, though still not looking at it.

"It's early, what are you doing pounding on my door?"

"This article." Mercy gestures to the phone now in Nari's hand. "It came out in America first, I think. Some group is basically saying that every single person who disappeared was like..." Mercy drifts off, the unsaid words heavy in the air between them.

Nari's stomach drops, her gaze snapping to the screen. She hurries to the couch, sitting with her eyes fixed on the phone as Mercy moves around the room, muttering softly to herself, flinging open the curtains to allow in the grey light of a cloudy morning.

A Global Purge of Sexual Predators – The Link Between the Disappeared Men

Nari's heart pounds in her chest as she scans the article. It reads like a scientific finding, a detached explanation of the information and methods used, its sterile tone somehow making the information even more captivating.

Mercy throws her purse on the chair and sits beside her on the couch, so close that Nari can feel her reading over her shoulder, her breath tickling the short hairs on Nari's neck. She shoots Mercy an annoyed look and scoots away an inch, scoffing as she hands Mercy back her phone.

"This is ridiculous." Despite her cool tone, Nari's heart is pounding out of her chest, unwilling to examine even the possibility of truth behind the words. Still, a wave of anxiety washes over her, and even though Mercy just arrived, all she wants is to be left alone to process this new information. Her fingers itching to snatch up her own phone left tangled in her sheets.

"The article was posted two days ago and has already been shared millions of times. It's viral global news. Loads of women are coming forward. Way bigger than any movement in the past."

It was clear what the article was insinuating. The common denominator – predators. Every single man who disappeared had either been convicted or was accused of sexual misconduct.

But Edward was not. He was perfect. He would never.

"Did he ever –"

"No!" Nari flushes, turning towards her with a violent glare, her heart kicking up at the irrational thought that Mercy might just be able to read her mind.

"He would never! We were going to get married!" Nari fumes at the idea. How could anyone think that about Edward. He was perfect.

Perfect.

Nari's gaze drifts down to the ring on her hand once more, her eyes lingering on the way even the grey light can capture every facet of the stones, casting tiny, shifting rainbows across the top of her hand.

"But I mean..." Nari looks up at Mercy's voice, her cheeks hot at the expression in her eyes. Mercy looks to be weighing her words, her eyes dancing down towards the impressive ring on Nari's finger. Mercy has never been one to shy away from speaking the truth, but for the first time she seems troubled, unsure.

"Have you talked to his family? You said they never got back to you. Did anyone finally call back?"

Nari had reached out to them right away. Though they had never met, Edward had told her time and time again that they knew all about her and were so excited to finally meet her. The few times they were scheduled for a dinner, something came up last minute. But his parents were busy and important, even distantly related to royalty Edward had once claimed.

After three unreturned calls to his mother (using a number she had procured online), Nari finally found his brother, one Edward had only rarely mentioned in passing. He was quite a few years older than Edward and had moved to America when Edward was still in secondary.

In her slightly frantic message, Nari explained that she was Edward's fiancé and couldn't get ahold of their parents. Asking if she could please have his mother or father's direct line. He had responded briefly that he was sorry he didn't know who she was, but he was grieving the loss of his brother *and* their father.

The news had shocked her. Nari had no idea his father had disappeared as well. Nari decided to give it a bit more time before trying again. So sure that once the fog of grief had cleared slightly, Edward's mother would reach out, would want to know her.

"She's busy! She's also grieving her husband, you know!" Nari hated the way Mercy flinched back at her words, immediately regretting her harsh tone.

"I know." Mercy's tone was calm and placating, and Nari couldn't help but turn her face away in shame.

Nari had scarcely been holding it together. If it wasn't for Mercy, the past three weeks would've been absolute hell. She was there after Edward had disappeared before her eyes, keeping her afloat throughout the fallout. They had stayed up all night to watch the news, huddled together as the world changed before their eyes. The beginning of samgyeopsal left abandoned on the stove.

At first, Mercy made a point of dragging Nari out a few times a week to volunteer around campus. In the wake of the disappearances, hundreds of students had left, returning home to deal with the immediate, heart-wrenching loss of family members and friends among the missing.

The two of them would take shifts in the library, at the help desk, attending the community building activities, even occasionally doing light groundskeeping work. Sometimes they'd venture into the city to assist at the women's relief center, set up to help those who had lost a primary caretaker in the household.

Mercy was like Nari in that she had no immediate plans to return home.

Nari had arrived at Cambridge ready to break from her shell, but unsure of how to take those first steps. Her family had been surprised when she hadn't chosen a college in America, but Nari thought America was a bit like an amusement park, fun for the first few hours, torture for the rest. When Nari had looked at the website for Cambridge, she was immediately taken with its old-world charm.

Mercy was in Nari's first class at Cambridge, and the sight of her long locs and glistening mocha skin captivated Nari immediately. She was a burst of color in a sea of neutral tones. Nari hadn't encountered any Kenyan women in her life, and in that moment she found herself unable to look away. It wasn't just her striking skin, her hair, or the vibrant clothes she wore. It was something deeper – the melodic cadence of her voice, the way she radiated warmth with every word, the constant smile that lit up her face. She spoke her mind without hesitation, without fear, and Nari couldn't help but be drawn to her bold, unfiltered energy.

Nari's hard expression fades into guilt and she can't help it as tears begin to fall from her eyes. Mercy sighs, pulling her into her chest, her hand coming to rest on the back of Nari's head as she begins to cry in earnest.

Nari settles against Mercy, relishing the familiar comfort of her warmth, her bright scent of verbena enveloping Nari, forcing her to push aside the pang of guilt at having wished just moments ago that Mercy would just leave her alone.

Mercy and Nari had been in the same English program since their freshman year, often finding themselves in the same classes and study groups. Their bond had been formed over late-night study sessions, discussions of literature, and ridiculous inside jokes that only the two of them truly understood. So, even when Edward came into Nari's life, Mercy was always there, a constant presence.

There was, of course, the natural chasm that tends to form when a friend enters a relationship – the unspoken distance that grows as priorities shift – but Mercy wasn't the kind of friend to let that change things. She understood that Nari's time was now divided, but she never held it against her. Even when Nari couldn't attend a party or activity, Mercy's response was always the same, "It's okay, next time!" And though they both knew that "next time" came less and less over the months, it didn't seem to matter. Mercy always had a way of making it feel like everything was just as it was before, as if nothing had really changed.

Edward had been deep into his chemistry studies, his days consumed by intense labs and rugby practice, leaving his schedule the complete opposite of Nari's.

Over time, she slipped into the rhythm of making herself available whenever he needed her – whether it was to grab a quick meal, rush off with him for the weekend to one of his matches, or spread her legs for him when he desired her comfort in the middle of the night. She never thought twice about how much she'd shaped her own life around his until he was gone from it.

When Mercy came over that night, rushing to her room less than an hour after his disappearance, Nari realized with a shock that Mercy hadn't been over to her place in months. They lived within the same complex, only minutes away, yet she couldn't even remember the last time she'd seen Mercy outside of class. How many times had she turned down an offer from Mercy to accommodate Edward's whims? Nari never thought twice about it. But watching Mercy, bent over in her small kitchen, sweeping up the glass remains of the OB lager bottles shattered across her floor, the grief had sharply twisted into guilt.

Nari could freely admit that she was enamored with Edward. She couldn't believe that he had chosen her.

The first time she saw him, her eyes had hardly stopped on his broad shoulders and flawlessly styled sandy blonde hair. He seemed like one of those too-perfect guys, the kind that were just pretty to look at from a distance, their perfect smiles and effortless charm belonging to some other world – one she wasn't even sure she belonged to.

So, Nari could hardly believe it when, an hour later, she caught him smiling at her from across the room. Mercy had wandered off long ago, and Nari had been content to sit back, nursing her warm beer, soaking in the ambient buzz of a typical college party. But then he was there – making his way toward her, a wide smile revealing perfectly white teeth, his light blue eyes practically glowing against the dark olive-green of his sweater, stretched tight across his arms and shoulders. He sat down beside her, and for a moment, she actually looked around, half-expecting there to be someone else sitting next to her, convinced that she must have been mistaken.

Nari knew she was pretty, but she had never been one to flaunt it. In South Korea, a feminist renaissance was stirring, challenging long-held societal expectations of women. But Nari's parents still carried a heavy weight of tradition, burdening her with expectations that had felt impossible to shake. After a year at Cambridge, and with Mercy's persistent encouragement, Nari had started to evolve beyond the girl she had been back home. Still, as she sat there, simply dressed in a soft white blouse and a pair of jeans, surrounded by girls in short designer dresses, perfect makeup, and effortless banter. She couldn't help but feel a bit out of place.

"Hi." That was all he needed to say. He knew it. She knew it. He knew that she knew it. His posh accent was a summons in itself. All she could do was smile, the flush on her pale skin the answer she never needed to utter.

On their one-month anniversary, Edward rented a car to drive them over an hour to Dotori, a popular Korean restaurant located near Finsbury Park station in London. It was small and charming, walk-in only, with small tables that lined the walls. It was simple and unpretentious. It felt like home. He seemed too good to be true.

"I know you miss him. I can't imagine how that must've felt, but you...I mean you told me he had secrets." Nari feels dizzy at her words, quickly pulling away from Mercy's embrace.

A few months after Edward and Nari got together, he was out of town for the weekend for a rugby match. Nari thought it would be fun to have a sleepover, just like they had during their freshman year when they were just two girls, so far from home, navigating a new world together. They stayed up late drinking, laughing, and reminiscing.

But when Mercy began asking a few probing questions about her relationship with Edward, Nari's composure cracked. It was a moment of weakness – one she now regrets. Nari shouldn't have opened her mouth, expressed her concerns, her worries about never meeting his parents, and the little moments here and there when something just didn't feel right. But despite the doubts, the green flags far outweighed the red, and Nari was desperately in love with him.

"Yes! I mean… maybe. But nothing like that!" Nari shoots back, indignant on his behalf.

"Of course not… but if you read it you'll see –."

"Please." Something in Nari's expression causes Mercy to stop, and she nods her head in acquiescence, a sad smile on her face.

"I'm sorry. You're right. This whole thing is an absolute mess. Did you want to go grab a bite? I'm going to head to the library in a little. Natalia mentioned meeting up later too if you're interested?"

Nari shakes her head, unable to stop her gaze from drifting down to the ring still on her finger. Edward had told her it was a family heirloom and passed down for generations. That his mother had given it to him to give to her. At the time, Nari didn't want to see the irregularity in it all. If it was a family heirloom, then wouldn't his mother have wanted to meet her first? There were so many parts of his life that she hadn't seen, but the parts she had seemed to be enough.

Nari walks Mercy to her door, promising a library shift with her tomorrow after workshop.

As soon as the door clicks shut, Nari is drawn to her computer, some unseen force guiding her as she settles onto her bed. The article is plastered everywhere, news reports from every major outlet covering its release, flooded with opinions, thoughts and feelings on the information now flooding in on each of the disappeared men.

Numerous articles discuss the various outages on the website, with server overloads as people rush to upload information on all the men whose profiles lack police reports or accusations. The sheer volume of data pouring in is overwhelming, a cascade of details, names, and faces all adding to a growing list that's quickly spiraling out of control.

With trembling hands, Nari navigates to the growing UK database and types his name and birthdate into the search field.

Nari lets out a gasp, unaware that she had been holding her breath as the page loaded. Dizzy nearly with relief that under his name are no further links – no mugshots, no convictions or complaints.

Edward had told her he believed in monogamous, long-term relationships, a sentiment that had initially caught her off guard. She was even more surprised when he admitted he had only been with one other person, his childhood girlfriend. But Edward wasn't just the polished, charming man she had once noticed across a room; he was so much more than his first impression. Beneath the surface was a depth she hadn't expected, a sincerity that made her believe in him.

Nari's brow furrows as her eyes land on a small notification beneath his name. She clicks on it, and a single comment is revealed, a lone message sitting starkly on the otherwise blank page.

'Took me years to see his charm was just a beautifully crafted mask disguising the hideous creature beneath.'

Day Forty-Five: Patsy – Chicago, Illinois

W as that the lawyer again?"

Patsy turns on the couch at the sound of the slam of the oven door, the scent of Heather's famous lemon blueberry muffins spilling from the kitchen and into the living room.

"Yup!" Patsy calls back, frustration clear in her voice. She groans, her head resting back against the couch, shutting her eyes as she tosses her cell phone on the cushion next to her.

"No progress then?" Patsy opens her eyes, Heather now standing over her, a plate with a muffin and a mug of coffee held out in offering. Patsy sends her a grateful smile, sitting up to accept them.

"No. Anne is still saying that there isn't sufficient evidence to reopen the case yet."

"Hmm, yeah. I mean, we kinda figured as much." Heather hums in thought, sitting down beside her.

"Yeah. Can't really just point to my article and be like 'look, all the guys who disappeared are predators,' so since my brother is still around – he's clearly innocent."

Heather barks out a dry laugh. "Shame."

Nobody besides Heather even knew she was the one behind it; all the members' identities were carefully protected. The group operated like something out of a movie – aliases, encrypted messages, and layers of digital safeguards to keep their identities hidden. They were a collective, each playing their part without ever fully knowing the others. Heather was the only one Patsy trusted with the full truth, though times like today, Patsy wishes there were others who knew as well.

Unfortunately, there hadn't been some new supernatural absolution clause added into the laws since the incident. She imagines her brother might not be the only one wrongly convicted of a sex crime, still sitting in their cells, clinging to the fragile hope that someone, somewhere, might believe in them enough to fight on their behalf. Patsy had moved beyond the guilt of abandoning her brother when he needed her most. She believed him now, believed him as she should have from the very beginning.

Now, she had a chance to do more than just believe. She had a chance to help him, to make others see the truth she had turned away from. No matter what the lawyer said about their limited options, she refused to give up. She would stop at nothing until her brother was free.

Patsy vetted five or six lawyers before she finally found the right one to take on Marcus's case. The process was exhausting, and the questions always started the same way. The first thing Patsy did was bring up the article – it was impossible not to, really. At that point, it had only been a few days since her data had been released to the public, yet it was already making waves across the globe, ruling headlines and sparking heated debates on every major news outlet and social media platform.

Patsy checked their reactions closely, scrutinizing every raised brow and careful word. She needed someone who not only believed in the gravity of her findings but also had the determination to navigate the legal system's labyrinthine complexities in this new age. This wasn't just a case for her, it was her brother's life, his future, and the vindication of the work she had poured many sleepless nights into. Each time a lawyer hesitated or dismissed the implications of the data, she politely ended the conversation and moved on, determined to find someone who was as unwavering in their conviction as she was.

As she had anticipated, the wealth of information about the disappeared continued to grow exponentially. Hackers, coders, and data analysts from around the globe joined forces, building upon the foundation she and the others had painstakingly laid.

What began as her personal investigation had snowballed into a worldwide effort. Every day, new findings about the disappeared emerged, some shocking, some validating what had already been suspected, and the collective effort took on a life of its own.

The majority of the public seemed to buy into the idea of this missing link, fueling a level of traffic to their website that no one had anticipated. Within the first days of the website going live, it had crashed multiple times, each outage throwing the system technicians and web administrators into a frenzy. They worked around the clock just to keep the site operational.

The data increased with every click, every search, and every comment left under a disappeared man's profile. Some posts were angry rants, others were tearful pleas for answers, and a few were nothing more than cold, hard truths tying the men to crimes they could no longer deny. Each contribution strained the system further, leaving the IT teams scrambling to expand server capacity faster than the demand could rise. But each time, the system was patched, the information preserved. It wasn't a court of law, it was something more – a court of public opinion.

Yet, there were still a few outliers, those who had lost husbands, brothers, or sons, best friends – many even with convictions – who couldn't reconcile the idea that their loved one had been a bad man. These were the people who would leave nasty comments under the article, baseless threats with nowhere to go.

So, it wouldn't be unusual to bring up the most talked-about news in the world with Marcus's potential lawyer, especially since her brother was in jail for the exact type of crime the article claimed had caused the men to disappear.

The first time around, everything moved too fast for them to fully comprehend what was even happening. Fear had controlled Marcus as he was cornered into accepting a plea deal. The men in the interrogation room had drilled him relentlessly, exploiting his fragile mental state to convince him that fighting back was pointless. They repeated the same threats over and over: the jury would take one look at the evidence and convict him without hesitation. But Patsy knew what they really meant when they told him that.

What ultimately broke him was the knowledge that the victim was a minor, not the seventeen she had told him, but only fifteen years old – an offense they told him could lead to a life sentence if the case went to trial.

Desperate to avoid the public spectacle and terrified of the consequences, Marcus signed the plea deal without consulting their mother, who was hell bent on fighting, appearing to have more faith in him than he had in himself. His court-appointed lawyer seemed indifferent, mindlessly shuffling through the papers as if Marcus's entire future wasn't hanging in the balance. There was no fight, no reassurance, just a hurried signature on a document that would define his life for years to come. Marcus agreed to serve eight years in prison. His lack of prior convictions and a few strong character references worked in his favor, but none of it softened the blow. Signing those papers felt like signing away his entire future.

The decision tore him, and their family, apart. Their mother had been furious with Patsy, unable to understand how Patsy could think for a second her brother would be capable of committing such crimes. But her mother didn't know how Patsy had spent most nights, tucked away in the basement, lifting rocks in the darkest corners of the web to see what lay beneath.

Marcus's version, and the truth, was that he met a girl at a party and had a completely innocent time with her. They had spent a few hours chatting, shared a kiss, exchanged socials and then split ways.

Marcus was freshly nineteen at the time, enjoying college and all that it had to offer, including the typical college party. Marcus wasn't a big drinker and had only been on his second beer of the night when she sat next to him around the bonfire. She was sweet, funny, and seemed wise beyond her years, with a dark, dry humor that matched Patsy's perfectly. She mentioned that her sister went to IU and she planned to join her the following year. They talked late into the night around the fire, passing a lukewarm beer back and forth as the flames crackled softly around them.

Long after everyone else had wandered off, they stayed behind, their conversation flowing easily as the night grew quieter. After sharing a few innocent kisses, she saw the time and panicked, taking off with vague promises to meet up again in the future.

The following Monday the police came to his classroom. The hall hushed as the uniformed officers stepped in, scanning the room of watchful eyes. One walked up to the professor, leaning in close, murmuring something into his ear. Marcus was just as curious as the rest of them, straining to hear what the officer was saying. It was only when the professor furrowed his brows and turned to Marcus that his heart dropped. The officers followed his gaze and began their way towards him. Marcus couldn't comprehend what was happening.

"Is everything ok?" Marcus thought of his mother, his sister. It had to have been bad if they were coming to collect him in the middle of class.

"Come with us, please." Marcus jumped into action, throwing his books and notes in his bag, quickly standing to follow. It was only when one of the men grabbed his arm that he turned to them in confusion. The whole class was watching. Marcus couldn't understand why they were dragging him like that. They wouldn't answer his questions, escorting him into a police car and directly off campus. He was left in a room for hours before someone finally told him why he was there, and the horrible crimes he had been accused of. Crimes that Marcus knew he would never in his life commit.

But Patsy could see clearly that someone was lying, and she knew now, without a shred of doubt, that it wasn't her brother. Since that first call, they had spent countless hours talking on the phone. Even in the thick of her research, running on no sleep and head aching from staring at the computer screen for countless hours, she always made time for him. He had poured his heart out, recounting every detail, every moment, until there was nothing left unsaid. Long before the data began to align so irrefutably, Patsy had already made up her mind to help him, to begin mending her wrongs.

When she began her investigation, one of the first things she discovered was that the man who had interrogated him, the one who played the role of bad cop in the police footage a bit too well, had vanished along with the rest of them. Ironic. The cop who had been pulling the strings, the one describing the poor victim's injuries in detail, the glint in his eyes now shining with a different light. Not determination to catch the 'bad guy', but his own true nature, hidden beneath his shiny badge and his practiced charming smile.

Even though Patsy had seen the worst of men, she never believed her brother was evil – had never blindly thrown him in with the worst of them. But she could admit to herself that, for a time, she'd thought he'd fallen off track. Maybe it had been a mistake, too much booze, the overwhelming college pressures, but it was one that had no appropriate justification and needed to be paid for.

She understood the demoralizing impact these crimes had on women, their sentences in court barely scratching the surface of the lifelong trauma left in their wake. Society, both men and women alike, often called victims liars when they dared to accuse wealthy or powerful men, claiming it was all for the money – as if any sum could ever fill the void left by the darkness those men had inflicted upon them.

Patsy was fortunate enough to have never experienced something like that herself – she was one of the lucky few. But she knew far too many women personally who had.

Just as people were now only one or two degrees away from the disappeared, Patsy had always been only one degree away from a woman who'd been sexually assaulted.

What her data showed more than anything was that the number of false claims women made about men paled in comparison to the countless ones that went unreported.

Going through Marcus's case files, Patsy realized she needed a third party, someone who could see things clearly. All the evidence could be manipulated, but the fact that he remained was the most damning piece of all.

So finally, she found Anne, a no-nonsense lawyer who believed wholeheartedly in the data and what it revealed. Anne was eager to take on Marcus's case and fight tooth and nail to get him out. But as with most legal battles, the situation was far more complex than it initially seemed.

The first issue was that the accuser, now seventeen, had only been fifteen at the time of the alleged incident. As she was still a minor, strict privacy protections surrounded her and her family, creating a treacherous ocean of legal barriers for Anne to navigate. These protections made accessing information about the case difficult without formal court intervention. Anne had submitted written inquiries to the District Attorney's Office and the local police station involved in the original investigation but had yet to receive any substantive response.

This led to the second, and biggest hurdle – the judicial system itself, which had decelerated to an even slower than normal crawl in the wake of the disappearances. Cases piled up, court dates were repeatedly delayed, and key officials – those still in place and those stepping in to replace the ones who disappeared – seemed perpetually overloaded, leaving Anne to navigate a system still bogged down by chaos and uncertainty.

Not only had a large portion of the prison population disappeared, so had the guards, cops, judges and lawyers. There were disappeared in every professional field, every religion and every race – though in America Patsy had not been too shocked to discover that a majority of disappeared had been white. Many upper-crust and not once convicted. A ledger with cash payouts kept hidden and tucked away.

But like everything else in the world, Patsy was surprised by how ordinary life continued to feel after such an extraordinary event. The world kept spinning. There were no apocalyptic riots, no bombs, no more mass shootings. There was no dramatic uptick in chaos everyone had been expecting – the kind of world-ending scenario so often depicted in movies, books, and TV shows, where society so easily crumbles into a dark, dystopian nightmare.

Instead, there was an odd sense of calm, almost surreal how the world just kept spinning. In countries with oppressive governments, women began to rise, no longer held back or silenced. Those woman stepped up, ready to reclaim their world. Finally, after years, no longer invisible. It was like a revolution, but not one of violence – it was one of strength and unity.

People were working again, easily getting back to their routines. More businesses were reopening, the streets slowly filling with life again, though much quieter, more peaceful. A few nights ago, Heather and Patsy had taken a late-night stroll around the neighborhood, and not once did they stop to look over their shoulders at every rustle or footfall.

Teachers were preparing for the upcoming school year, sorting through lesson plans and gathering supplies, trying to build some sense of normalcy.

Heather had even designed a necklace after the article's release – a delicate gold pendant of Kali, the Hindu goddess of destruction and transformation, liberation, empowerment, and love. Kali embodied both fierce strength and nurturing motherhood, breaking chains and paving the way for freedom. The necklace sold like crazy, and before long, their roles had completely shifted.

With Patsy's company still closed and her side projects now slowed down, the momentum Heather had gained from the sales was undeniable.

Patsy found herself pulling Heather out of her studio late into the night, a constant stream of coffee, tea and sandwiches appearing at random hours of the day. It was the least she could do after Heather had catered to her during those long days and sleepless nights, supporting her through every twist and turn of the investigation. Now, it was time to return the favor, even if it was just with small gestures.

It appeared that many seemed to find explanation and solace in their chosen higher power. Especially after the article was released, it seemed to solidify that this had been some sort of divine intervention. That women were being given their first real chance.

The panel of experts had been disbanded, though there were still those trying to find some sort of scientific explanation. These days they were mostly fantastical claims, printed in tabloid magazines or side-column blurbs on a news website.

"Secret NASA Mission – Men Sent to Mars!"

"The Missing Men: Time Travelling Incident Gone Wrong."

Patsy's favorite claim, and the one she enjoyed believing the most, was that it was a mass alien abduction. People claimed these higher beings had come down to cleanse the Earth. People ran all sorts of directions with this theory; humans really did have limitless imagination. Patsy had even come across a fanfiction where the disappeared men were dragged to an off-planet prison by aliens, only to wake up as the very women they had mistreated on Earth. Patsy had left a 'kudos' on this one.

"But you have the girl's name finally, right?" Patsy glances over at Heather, grimacing as she nods in confirmation. She hadn't exactly gotten her information through legal means. The collective had easily found the girl, though Patsy was unwilling to turn the information over to Anne, knowing that there wasn't much she could do with it that would hold up in court. She would only tell Anne if things went how she hoped.

"Yeah… but, I dunno. Just worried this might go tits up and it'll just make an even bigger mess of things."

"But if you could convince her to come forward and tell the truth, they'd have to let him out. Right?"

That was only partially true. Recantation wasn't an automatic get out of jail free card. There were still legal processes that would have to be followed. But Patsy knew that it would speed things up to have the victim set the record straight.

It was only another six months until the victim was eighteen. At that point it would be easier to get in contact with her. At the same time, Patsy didn't want to wait any longer. Even though he'd only been in prison for two years, he had lost so much of his life already. She could hear it in his voice every time they spoke on the phone.

Though prison had gotten much better since the disappearances, finally well below the capacity line at which it danced for decades, it wasn't the place for Marcus. He deserved freedom, another chance at life.

"I don't think it would be that easy. But I know the second mom arrives she will want a full report… and will be bitter there isn't better news."

"Why do you think I made her favorite muffins?"

Patsy's mother had been overwhelmed with emotion when she told her she was reopening Marcus' case, that she had found a lawyer and was determined to bring him home. Patsy broke down right along with her, the guilt of leaving him out in the cold for so long still a heavy weight on her shoulders. But she was determined – she couldn't change the past, but she could fight for his future – no matter how long it took or how difficult the road ahead might be.

Patsy was so confident in his innocence and her ability to bring him home, that she and Heather already set up a room for him in their house. This decision led to a heated debate with her mother, who was adamant that Marcus should come home to her instead. Patsy knew the argument wasn't over yet – her mother wasn't one to back down easily. But in the end, the choice was his.

Even so, her mother was just relieved to see Patsy stepping up for her brother, to see the family beginning to heal after so many fractured years. And though Patsy knew her mother wouldn't admit it outright, deep down she was happy too – happy that her son might finally come home, happy that her children might rebuild the bond they'd once had. The prospect of seeing them close again, after everything, was a comfort neither of them had dared hope for in a long time.

Later that night, Patsy sits in her office, opening the file she had revisited countless times since it appeared in her inbox. A picture of a pretty girl with dirty blonde hair and a strained smile pops up in the corner, and for the hundredth time, she reads through the details.

Her mother had been exactly how she expected, frustrated and unable to comprehend why Marcus wasn't home already. Heather patiently tried to remind her that the courts were still catching up, that these kinds of proceedings could take a while.

"Yeah well, my neighbor Justin, you know? His cousin Martha said that her daughter's boyfriend was able to get this special exception and have his case totally dropped because the accuser had disappeared! They should know by now! Marcus should be out with the rest of them!"

Patsy bit her tongue, stopping herself from snapping back in frustration. Heather's hand on her knee served as a steadying reminder, a silent plea for patience. The worst part, though, was that she agreed with her mother. There had been too much happening in the world, too many headlines and crises, for anyone to spare a thought for convicted sex offenders still sitting in prison. Patsy knew the number was likely small, infinitesimal even. And that was precisely the problem. It was so small, so insignificant in the grand scheme of things, that it had probably been completely overlooked.

But Patsy had kept her mother appraised of everything the lawyer told her. She knew just as well as Patsy did the various routes – and the obstacles – there were to Marcus's freedom. They knew that they needed new evidence to reopen the case, and Patsy's article wasn't considered evidence in a court of law.

Patsy could tell that Marcus was trying to be patient, but after receiving more bad news from Anne last week, she could tell he was at his breaking point.
"Please Pats, you've gotta find her. She will come clean. She has to now. I just know it. Please find her."

Though Patsy had never openly admitted her work to him the way she had to Heather, he seemed to know she was especially skilled at finding information – and sometimes, she suspected he knew even more than he let on.

All Marcus had was her first name but finding her was an easy task once Patsy gained access to his social media accounts. It was the reaching out to her that was hard. Patsy had done many illegal and legally-grey things over the years in the pursuit of justice, she only had to convince herself that this was one of them.

Patsy clicks on the link attached to her file and a new blank email window pops up on the screen.

Taking a deep breath, Patsy begins the message she's thought of writing time and time again.

> *Hi Keira,*
> *My name is Patsy. I'm so sorry to have to reach out, but need your help...*

Day Forty-Six:
Keira – Martinsville, Indiana

M omma!" Keira shuts the front door, tossing her keys on the side table and kicking off her shoes.

Keira calls out again, following the soft sound of Fleetwood Mac, Stevie Nicks' sultry voice guiding her through the house.

"Out here baby!" her mother calls from the back porch, the music growing louder with each step of her approach.

Keira pushes open the screen door and stops at the sight of her mother, a warmth rushing through her that pulls her mouth into a smile.

Everything about the scene before her is a stark reminder of their freedom.

Her mother stands halfway up the ladder, her torso disappearing behind the edge of the porch roof as she wrestles with something unseen in the gutters. The chunky knit sweater she wears has hitched up slightly, exposing a sliver of pale skin above the waistband of her loose jeans that are tucked into a pair of oversized and worn work boots.

A woman completely transformed.

Her mother hears the slam of the screen door and peeks down over the edge, shooting Keira a wide smile.

"These gutters were sagging. It's been bothering me for months!"

"Let me help!" Keira walks down the porch steps, craning her neck to get a look at what her mother is up to as the drill whirs to life.

"No need." Her mother shoots her a proud smile as she wriggles the gutter, testing its steadiness.

"See, all done." She hands Keira the drill and comes down the ladder, wiping her dirty hands on her jeans with a satisfied grin. Around her are piles of leaves, their yard bin dragged out from the garage and stuffed to the brim.

"Here let me." Keira tries to help as her mother begins to pick up the other tools, haphazardly placed around the floor. It's Keira's first instinct to make sure all the tools are put away properly, nothing out of place, but her mother gently pushes her aside.

"No baby, please just take a load off. You thirsty? There's sweet tea in the fridge." Her mother tosses the rest of the tools in the tool bag and slumps into one of the wicker chairs on the porch, kicking off the large boots as her feet find the matching wicker glass-top table that's graced this back porch for as long as Keira could remember.

"Yeah, ok. You want some more?" Keira motions to the near empty glass beside her mom.

"Sure, sweetie." Keira picks up her glass and walks back into the house, turning as she shuts the screen door behind her to find her mom looking up at her work with a satisfied gleam in her eyes.

Last week Keira had come home to find her mother on the riding mower, a wide smile on her face as she weaved back and forth across their large backyard, her hair loose and wild in the wind.

Keira's mom had always dressed like a conservative churchwoman: neutral-toned button-up dresses that fell to her calves, thin, unflattering cardigans, and plain dress flats. Her wardrobe was a testament to her submission, her enslavement to the man who called himself her husband.

But seeing her now is like witnessing a transformation. Keira never truly realized how young her mother was. She'd been only nineteen when she got pregnant with Keira, but the years had worn her down, molding her into something beyond recognition. A woman her mother no longer recognized when she looked in the mirror.

Now, she sits with her legs casually crossed and propped on the table, her hair loosely braided with soft wisps framing her face, a few stray leaves caught in the strands. Her cheeks glow pink from the sun and the work, her eyes bright and alive in a way Keira has never seen. The shoulders that once hunched in quiet despair now rest easily, and her gaze that had always been cast downward, now meets Keira's with confidence, her eyes full of a youthful curiosity and wonder.

Keira can't believe she had thought her mother was broken, that there was nothing left of her. She had truly believed her father had stripped her mother down and left her with nothing. But in his wake, the pieces somehow found their way back steadily, day by day. It wasn't an easy journey for the two of them, but now, less than two months after her father had disappeared, they were better than ok, in fact, better than she ever thought they could be. They were living in the fantasy that Keira had been dreaming about for years.

The days and weeks that followed his disappearance, and that of over two billion men across the globe, felt a bit like a blur.

For over a week they didn't leave the house, the two of them on autopilot, listening to the radio and news. Huddled around it in shock, waiting for every little update, a shared fear that neither could voice – what if he came back.

During the day, her mother had been skittish, every little noise causing her to flinch, a reflex born from years of fear. The ingrained terror clung to her, refusing to let go even in the light of freedom.

At night, Keira would wake from nightmares, her father's face hovering above her, the oppressive weight of his presence lingering in her mind. It would take her several long moments of sitting upright, scanning the room, and double checking the news on her phone for reassurance before she could convince herself that he was truly gone.

Those early nights Keira would calm her panicking heart, only to hear her mother's soft sobs from her room down the hall. For the first week Keira left her, so caught up in her own anguish. It was overwhelming to suddenly have to shuffle through years of abuse with no warning, the floodgates torn open all at once.

Escaping this kind of trauma wasn't just a singular event, but an entire process of acceptance and healing that took years. Keira and her mother hadn't been planning some amazing escape; they hadn't even yet mustered the mental fortitude to consider doing so.

These were thoughts Keira kept locked away deep, her few hundred dollars that she kept under the floorboards hardly a declaration of an attempt. Their freedom had come without warning, and the aftermath had left them feeling scared and unsure. They were like animals kept in a cage for so long that, even when the door swung open, they hesitated, unsure of how to step out or what freedom might even look like.

But this was something wholly different. Because normally, even after a woman left or got away from her abuser, the trauma always lingered. Fear that he might come back, that he wasn't truly gone, because he could so easily be replaced by someone else.

But now, in their new world, women were the overwhelming majority. And that thought alone fueled something in Keira as she sat up the eighth night in a row, waking from nightmares to hear the sound of her mother's sobs. The news stated plainly, over two billion men disappeared in a day. He was gone, and Keira knew with overwhelming certainty that he was not coming home.

When she pushed open the door to her mother's bedroom, she was not shocked to see her face red, tear streaked and splotchy with grief. It was a face she'd seen many times before. But there was something different to these tears, the anger and determination glimmering in the depths of her expression. Before her were her father's things, all packed away in bags and boxes. Keira hadn't even thought of what it must be like to sleep in this room surrounded by his possessions, the nightmares that her mother must have been waking from, and how much longer it took each night for her to realize that she was free.

"I didn't want you to see this." Her mother crumbled at Keira's soft touch, her face falling into her hands as if that could hide the clear anguish in her expression.

"See what?"

"I'm so weak," her mother wailed, the sobs starting anew. "I never wanted this, you know? This was never what I saw for myself." She seemed to be full of thoughts and feelings, finally given permission to express them, bursting out of her with every sob.

"I know." Keira didn't really, but she *could* understand. Years earlier, during a brief stage of rebellion, Keira had found a dusty box in the attic while looking for a place to hide things she didn't want her father to find. The box was full of pictures of her grandparents and mother's childhood, images of the house during its various stages of production. Kiera had found her mother's high school yearbook, and in that moment she realized she had never seen pictures of her mother before her father had changed her. She had only really remembered her one way. It was almost like looking at another version of herself, youthful and so full of life. Her mother had no idea of the life that was in store for her.

"It's funny how badly I want to erase him, even though he's already gone.... But, it's different from death. At least with death, there's closure. But this, it's just –." Her mother trailed off, clutching a crumpled tissue in her hand as she wiped at her dripping nose.

"He may be gone, but the shame is still here." Her mother pressed her fist to her chest with a loud thump, bits of the frayed tissue landing on her lap.

Keira knew what she was referring to, she carried the same shame, though she understood it was different.

"I should've done more." The words were barely a whisper, her eyes fixed on the floor. Keira had known this conversation would surface eventually, but she couldn't help the dread that crept in at the words. The week had passed in a careful, unspoken truce, their conversations limited to news headlines and how the world beyond their walls was changing – never how it had changed them.

"I heard Mrs. Watson's son is gone too. He'd just finished high school, was about to head off to college."

"The pastor, can you believe it! He'd been at the church for near forty years!"

It was always someone else. Some locals, a celebrity, billionaire or politician. There was so much speculation as to why, but they didn't ponder on that, using the news to keep their minds busy and away from their own problems.

Unlike many, they didn't immediately call the police, frantic and begging for help in finding him. It wasn't until a day later that an alert came through the news, stating that due to an overwhelming surge of emergency calls, a form had been created online for individuals to report their missing loved ones.

In that quiet moment, they exchanged a look, and without a word, Keira pulled her phone from her pocket and typed in the web address. Two minutes later, they returned to watching the news.

But at night the demons would come out to play, each piece of clothing or picture a reminder of their captor who had taken over their home and robbed them of their life.

"Please, Mom." Keira's voice trembled. She wasn't sure she had it in her to rehash the past. Apologies wouldn't change anything now. She knew her mother loved her – that she'd been trapped in an impossible situation. But love hadn't made it easier. Now she was the one asking please.

There were those years, not so long ago, when Keira pushed the limits, daring her father to act, even though a part of her knew he had none. Maybe it had been a death wish. Maybe she thought if he killed her, it would finally be over, her mother set free as her father was carted off to jail. But every time, she came back home to her mother, bruised but still breathing.

Maybe her mother had poured whatever strength she had left into Keira. Maybe it was Keira's duty to nurture that spark, to hold onto it until she could pass it back to the woman who had given it to her.

"No, baby. I have to." The look in her mother's eyes stole Keira's breath. A fierceness and determination she'd never seen before. Keira could only nod in response.

"I was a lot like you when I was younger. Fierce, determined, so alive. I'd like to think that your father stole it all from me, but the truth was, I gave it away. I see now.

"We had only been together a few months before I'd gotten pregnant with you. So, we got married; it was the only thing to do at the time. My momma never liked him, but he was a charmer at first… Gosh, baby the look in your eyes the first time he slapped me...the shock on your face." Tears bloomed anew in her eyes, trickling down her face.

"I didn't know what he was up to with you until after it had already begun." The shame in her mother's eyes was so strong that Keira had to look away, pushing down the memories that threatened to break free.

"By then, I was so broken. One night, your father woke up to find me sitting over him. I'd been watching him, contemplating his death. I couldn't stop thinking about how easy it might be to end it all. To poison his dinner or suffocate him while he slept. But when he opened his eyes, I knew I couldn't.

"He told me time and time again, that if I did anything, he'd kill you. That he could get away with it because he was buddies with half the force. That it would be too easy to hide a body on the property or shove me down the stairs and call it an accident. Then you'd be left alone with just him and that thought –." Her mother broke into a fresh fit of sobs, and Keira wasn't surprised to find tears streaming down her own cheeks.

That night, Keira took her mother back to her own room where they fell asleep wrapped around each other in her small twin bed.

She forgave her mother. The only way to heal was to move forward. What was done was done. The past couldn't be erased, only acknowledged. People often became trapped in their yesterdays, replaying what they could've done differently or better. But that was a dead end, a worthless pursuit.

This was their chance – a moment they could step into the future together.

The next morning Keira helped her mother remove any trace of their father from the entire house. They loaded up every bag, box, stray shoe or jacket into the back of his old pick-up truck.

Every toss from the front porch into his truck was cathartic. By midday she and her mother were covered in a sheen of sweat and laughing, making a game out of seeing how far they could throw the lopsided bags into the bed of the truck.

When the truck was fully loaded, her mother looked at her, a mischievous smile pulling at her mouth. "Should we dump this and pick up some dinner?"

Over the course of the day, they had seemed to forget why they were throwing all of his stuff in the truck in the first place. Their house was on the outskirts of town, closer to Paragon than Martinsville, where their closest neighbor was a few dirt roads or a thick copse of trees away. But it didn't take too long for them to remember. A few minutes later they were pulling onto the bypass, the stark reminder immediately clear. A few abandoned cars on the side of the road, their local church with a sign hanging in memoriam for the pastor and the others missing from their town.

Still somehow, it hadn't dampened their mood, made them want to turn back. If anything, it confirmed the weight of the truth that sat in the back of the truck.

Martinsville had always been a small town, but overnight it felt as though it had shrunk even further. They stayed up to date through the local news and social media websites, yet beyond posts on the community page grieving missing loved ones, there had been little in the way of major incidents in their town.

There was a National Guard outpost in Martinsville, so their remaining members quickly mobilized. Aside from an incident at the local lumber mill, where a few employees disappeared mid-shift, causing an accident that led to minor injuries, the town faced the usual car accidents seen across the country. As a highway town situated right between Indianapolis and Bloomington, Martinsville experienced its share of pileups, but the roads were cleared efficiently. People were no longer commuting, their usual busy highway mostly quiet save for the occasional local traffic.

The town had lost its sheriff as well as a few of its local police, but there didn't seem to be the crime or chaos one might have expected. It was mostly quiet, families grieving and trying to make sense of something unexplainable.

Some of the larger businesses and chain restaurants remained closed, but one of the local bars in town had opened its doors, offering food, drinks, and a sense of community for residents seeking solace and connection. Not much different than it always had been. Except when Keira and her mother walked through the door, it was mostly women who made up the customers instead of men.

Keira couldn't quite shake the novelty of it all. Sitting in a bar eating greasy food while her mother enjoyed a few beers, listening as the neighbors talked around them.

From what they heard, the National Guard had been planning to make rounds confirming the disappeared and gathering a new census, not just here, but all across the country.

Keira was pulling onto their long dirt road when she realized they'd never even dumped her father's things. Instead, she turned at the last minute, taking them to the edge of the property where her father had made their burn pile for years.

That night, they stood around the fire watching the last remnants of her father turn to ash.

A few days later a man and woman from the National Guard showed up at their door, and after a five-minute interview, the woman handed them a card loaded with one thousand dollars, and they went on their way, offering condolences and the promise of more aid in the near future.

The next week stores opened back up; the townspeople had money to spend. Ten days after her father and the other men disappeared, Keira was asked if she'd like to resume work at the diner.

At the end of her first day at work, she came home to find her mother dressed in those now-familiar jeans and old t-shirt, the cream-colored walls of her mother's bedroom now a pale green.

"What do you think?" Keira was too shocked to respond, like meeting a version of her mother she had never met before. A spark of life behind her eyes.

It progressed from there, each day Keira returning from work to find something new. On the days she didn't work, she'd help her mom pull down old curtains and bedding, working their way through each room and making small changes until the space felt new.

On the nights Keira was home she'd have dinner with her mother, and they'd snuggle up on the couch together watching old reruns of their favorite shows. Hollywood wouldn't be up and running for a while, but thankfully they were both fans of the classics.

Slowly, this dream that Keira had for the two of them began to take shape.

Day twenty was a setback.

When Keira came downstairs mid-morning, having worked the late shift, her mother was sitting on the back porch, feet tucked beneath her as she stared off into the yard towards the large black spot where the last of her father's remains had turned to ashes.

Her mother hid the pain and trauma for so many years, but now the whole world knew. Nobody could hide any longer it seemed. It was everyone's burden to share, not just their own. Everyone's dirty laundry had been aired at once.

It was like the world was collectively moving through the stages of grief, taking one step forward then two steps back. Just when people started to move into Depression and Acceptance, many flew right back to Denial. But it was a different denial, not that the men were gone, but that they could no longer stay propped on the pedestals in which they had been placed.

The article had stated plainly that they were all abusers. Interestingly enough, her first thought was of the banner outside church. How long would it be until someone took it down.

That night Keira and her mother shared a drink for the first time. She had been surprised when her mother pulled down two glasses, the dusty bottle of whiskey that had been set aside and untouched since that fateful day, uncorked and drained between their cups.

The drinking wasn't about numbing pain or rehashing the past, but acceptance. Who cares if everyone knew – they were no longer alone. There were millions of other women out there who lost their husbands, sons, brothers and partners. Some they didn't even know were abusive, which Keira thought might have even been worse. At least her father never wore a mask around them; they saw his true face clearly. It wasn't hidden behind soothing words or slipped off as soon as he left home.

The next morning over breakfast, her mother brought up the idea of going back to college. It had always been her dream to study English and become a librarian. Keira's grandmother had been one, and for a time, her mother imagined herself tucked away behind those same towering stacks of books where she spent so many days of her youth, finding solace in the pages of novels, discovering new worlds. The thought had always lingered in the back of her mind, but life, as it often does, had pulled her in different directions. Now, it seemed like a possibility again – something she could finally pursue, even if it meant starting over.

Slowly again they progressed, moving back into the stage of acceptance. Each time Keira came home to find her mother lost in a book or sweating over a project. The house, the future, was theirs again.

Keira fills their cups with tea and heads back out to the porch. Her mother's head is back against the edge of the seat, eyes closed peacefully. She doesn't open them until Keira sets down her glass on the table.

"What do you want for dinner tonight? You hungry?"

"Not really. Had something at work."

"Well, I was thinking of trying this recipe I found online," her mother says, a knowing smile pulling at her lips.

Keira laughs. She's heard those words countless times over the past two weeks.

Her father had always had specific meal requests, ones Keira couldn't stand. Her mother would dutifully make him pan-seared pork chops, boxed mashed potatoes, and canned corn a few nights a week, their metallic taste lingering in her mouth long after the meal was over. Other times, it was Velveeta mac and cheese, the kind with the powdered cheese packet, mixed with browned ground beef and a side of canned green beans that came in that slimy, over-salted broth. Sometimes it was frozen meatloaf from a box, mashed potatoes with instant gravy, or the dreaded tuna casserole, the one her mother made when she was too tired to cook. Over-processed, bland, disgusting crap – food that had been shoved into his mouth for years.

Every morning, her mother would be up early, fixing him a bologna and American cheese sandwich to toss in his lunch box with chips and a couple of those prewrapped cherry pies and a soda. It had been her mother's routine for as long as she could remember.

But now, with her father gone, things had changed. His rules and routines no longer held any weight in their lives. Her mother was rediscovering herself. It was like she was a teenager again – everything felt new, fresh, and exciting. Keira couldn't say she regretted showing her mother Pinterest. It seemed like every day there was a new project in the works.

"So, what are we having this time?"

Her mother laughs and kicks a sock-covered foot out towards Keira in a playful gesture.

"You'll love it, I promise!" With that her mother scoops up the shoes and walks into the house.

"We need to get you some proper work boots now that you're the official handyman of the house," Keira teases, rising to follow her mother.

Her mother laughs, pouting down at the shoes, as she places them on the rack by the back door.

"They were my daddy's. Can't get rid of them. But you're right. Anyway, we should head to town soon."

"Oh yeah? What do you need?"

"I wanted to pick up the next batch of books off my list from the library. Thought we could try that cute spot in town too. I heard they opened back up."

"Sure." Keira takes a seat at the kitchen table, her fingers grazing the smooth wood, barely noticing the small dent on one side. The one left from her father's last tirade. His anger had left its mark on nearly everything it touched, but now the dent seemed almost insignificant, a small, faded memory of a man who had been an unrelenting force in their lives. His hold on their lives sanded away, devoid of its once painful bumps and ridges.

Keira pulls out her phone as her mother begins moving around the kitchen pulling out ingredients.

"Figured I would start now because it takes a while. Have you ever had homemade pasta?"

"Huh? Um no, I don't think so. Can't imagine Olive Garden counts."

She scrolls through her social media as her mother works away. Finally, she goes to her email, scrolling

half-heartedly through the numerous messages, her
eyes barely grazing over the junk mail and news alerts.
Her eyes stumble on an unfamiliar name, curiosity
getting the better of her as she clicks into the message,
her breath catching as she reads the first few sentences.

"You may remember my brother Marcus..."

Day Seventy-Five: Zarmina – Herat, Afghanistan

Zarmina looks up from the papers on her desk at the recognizable shuffle of feet from around the corner. A second later, she is greeted by Shahar's smiling face, her brow shiny from perspiration as she sets down a pile of fresh sheets on the desk next to Zarmina's.

"Have the rooms been prepared?" she asks without looking up from the papers spread on the desk before her.

"Yes. The new girls should be arriving within the hour."

"Ok. Take a rest friend, it's going to be a long day." Zarmina motions to the chair beside her as she examines the checklist in her hand, crossing another item off the list.

With the work they began doing, Zarmina quickly realized she would need an office, so the two of them took over the prison director's space. Pictures of regime leaders removed and replaced with newspaper cuttings, the guns that lined the wall tossed in a bin and removed, replaced with tapestries and dried flowers. The grey, smoke-stained sealed windows now clean and broken open, sound drifting up from the sweeping courtyard below.

"Have you thought more about the offer? We will be at full capacity again soon."

"Briefly, yes." Zarmina sighs and stands, walking to the window.

Below her, women are a bustle of movement, and Zarmina observes them as they work, their hands neat and practiced as they hang beautifully woven textiles in shimmering hues of gold, indigo, and crimson. Each piece of fabric ripples in the early morning breeze, catching the sunlight and casting colorful reflections on the dirty, barren ground. Nearby, other women carefully lay out rows of intricate jewelry on soft cloths – the etched silver bangles, beaded necklaces, and dangling earrings glinting with promise.

The once depressing yard the women used to shuffle in, heads bent low and voices hushed, has been completely transformed, bustling with life and energy, a vibrant bazaar sprung to life. Every corner is filled with something to draw the eye: vibrant scarves fluttering, delicate glass bottles catching light, baskets overflowing with fragrant spices. The air is thick with the scent of freshly brewed chai, its earthy aroma mingling with the sweet scent of jalebi frying in bubbling oil.

Laughter and chatter bubble up around her as the women move gracefully through the space, their heads held high with pride and purpose. They tease one another, voices filled with affection, occasionally erupting into loud giggles. Zarmina finds their joy contagious, her mouth pulling into a wide smile at the view.

Zarmina studies the women, a majority have their hijabs loosely draped, their soft edges falling just so, while others let their hair cascade freely, thick and lustrous in the sunlight.

For a moment, she's lost in it.

What a novel thought that something so simple as enjoying another women's splendor so freely could hold so much weight. Was it a sin for other women's beauty to be recognized?

Zarmina recalls, as a child, the first time she saw a group of women walking down the street, their bodies completely covered in black burqas, the mesh slit concealing their eyes. She must have seen them before – though such a sight was rare in the city during that time – but this was the first time it truly caught her attention. The women she'd seen before fully veiled had been dressed in beautiful burqas, light blue fabric intricately inlayed with silver threading and small gemstones that caught the light.

There were pictures in her childhood books of princesses veiled and covered in these beautiful gowns. But there was something unsettling about seeing it then, the way their faces were hidden beneath all that black, their identities obscured. For a fleeting, terrifying moment, she wondered if the women could even see through the fabric. Beneath all that cloth, they could have been anyone – each piece of their femininity and identity tucked away, swallowed by the darkness.

As they passed the women, she turned to her mother, her eyes taking in the fashionable flowy blouse and slacks her mother often wore, her colorful hijab loosly framing her beautiful face.

"Why are those women dressed like that?"

Her mother turned at Zarmina's question, her eyes easily spotting the women huddled together on the street. So out of place among the more modern fashion that had taken the city by storm the last few years. Something in her mother's expression shifted slightly, and Zarmina remembers how that look had made her heart slightly race. But her mother turned back, her expression calm as she answered, "Because it makes them feel safe."

Her mother had said it so casually, as if it begged no further explanation, but it had only brought a thousand more questions to the surface.

"Do you feel safe?" Zarmina's hand felt clammy clamped tightly in her mothers. She stopped walking then, dropping Zarmina's hand to rest hers lightly on her shoulders.

"Yes, my love. But..." She seemed to think, her eyes scanning Zarmina's face. It was as if her mother was searching for something more than the child that stood before her, but the woman she would someday become.

Her mother was a professor of social sciences at Kabul University, and had been among the women fighting for rights for women in Afghanistan during the fifties and sixties – rights that at that time in her life, Zarmina hadn't even considered. Their house was often filled with artists, thinkers, activists, the kind of modern women who filled the capital at that time, who wore skirts, their hair pinned into buns on the top of their head, their lipstick leaving bright marks on the rims of their glasses.

After a moment of contemplation her mother responded. "Things are different outside the city. Our world isn't very safe for women, so sometimes it is best not to be seen at all."

Zarmina wanted to push. Unsafe how? How could the world be unsafe for her just because of what she looked like? Just because of the body in which Allah placed her.

Her mother didn't bring up the conversation again for another six years. She had known deep down that at some point they would have to flee the city with war and unrest on the horizon. Her mother had seen the foundation of Kabul and their country, and all of it's progress, begin to crumble. Many nights Zarmina could hear the hushed frantic whispers between her parents, the dinner parties that once Zarmina could attend, now taking place after she was supposed to be tucked into bed, the mood cautious and somber.

The topic came up again when her mother asked, "Why is it that you wear the hijab?" Zarmina had always been taught it was worn as a sign of faith. It is not just the scarf itself but what it symbolized.

"To show my faith...and for modesty," Zarmina responded earnestly. She felt she dressed modestly, her knee length dresses over a pair of loose pants, her hair tied back and kept covered by her large collection of colorful scarves.

"Yes, my love. And what do you think modesty means?"

"The Quran tells us that modesty is about humility, inner purity, self-respect."

"Yes, you are right. But there are many who believe it is much more for a woman, that women are below men."

Zarmina looked at her mother at that, her brows furrowed in confusion. Her mother and father had been teaching her from the Quran for years that women and men were equal under God.

'O mankind! Be conscious of your Lord, who created you from a single soul, and from it created its mate, and from the two of them spread countless men and women.'

Her mother used to tell her that, according to Allah, men and women were split from the same soul, equally rewarded for their good deeds and righteousness.

"I fear I did not teach you enough about the world beyond these city walls." Her mother looked pained, remiss.

Zarmina was so naive then, and that bubble popped suddenly and violently.

It wasn't many years later that Zarmina found herself draped in the same black burqa as the women she had once watched in the streets. She had become one of them – a woman hidden away, her bruises concealed beneath the folds of fabric, her slow, measured steps masking the pain her husband inflicted day and night. She knew that not every woman who covered herself lived under the same shadow, but she couldn't help but wonder how many did.

How many endured in silence? How many had been conditioned by fear for so long that they no longer recognized what had been taken from them?

But it was always on us as women, always our fault. We were the ones who had to cover up, to shrink ourselves, to stay hidden as a means of protection.

Why was it our responsibility to avoid harassment, instead of theirs not to harass?

An article from America had spread like wildfire a few months ago, and it wasn't long before it reached Zarmina's hands. An anonymous group had claimed that every single man who had vanished had a history of abusing women.

Zarmina wasn't shocked – many in her country, along with others under war-torn, regime-controlled rule, had lost countless men. But what surprised people was the sheer scale of it elsewhere. The numbers in America were just as staggering with eighty million men gone.

It wasn't just an Afghanistan problem. It wasn't just *their* culture. Their crimes against women had simply been more visible, more openly enforced. But in America? Their sins were just better hidden.

People in the West could look at pictures of women in burqas and shake their heads, talking about how oppressed they were. But women in their own countries lived under the same ever-present shadow, just in different clothing.

Looking down at the courtyard, that world feels like a distant memory.

"Hard to imagine leaving here after everything." Zarmina startles at Shahar's voice from beside her, similarly watching the scene below.

"But you are right," Zarmina agrees. "The number of women pouring in compared to those leaving, we won't be able to host many more soon enough."

Newly appointed officials arrived at the prison gates just a week after Herat's new governor, Roya Fayez, had taken office. A small group had come to check on the prison, offering all of the women amnesty and a chance to start over. In the days leading up to their arrival, Zarmina and Shahar spent long nights with the other women, trying to determine their next steps before the knock at the gates inevitably came.

They had known it was only a matter of time, each day the news reported more and more progress taking place outside their walls.

What Zarmina realized more than anything was that many of these women had nowhere else to go. Some had no one left to return to, while others came from deeply conservative backgrounds and feared the world outside, unsure of how to rebuild their lives or where to go next.

So, when the time came, Zarmina stepped forward as their representative. She explained everything to the officials – the women who had left, those who had chosen to stay, and the uncertainty they all collectively faced. Most importantly, she made her case: the prison should remain an open refuge, a place for other women in the city and beyond with nowhere else to go.

It didn't take long for food and supplies to arrive, with the governor granting Zarmina and the others their wish and full support.

The women wasted no time getting to work, and word quickly spread about the prison that had transformed into a refuge.

From there, the momentum only grew. Every week, there was a knock at the door – sometimes a woman from a humanitarian group wanting to offer her medical assistance, social workers from NGO's who were in the country helping women who were still dealing with trauma, an Alimah from the local mosque who came to talk about women's rights in Islam, other times, just a mother and daughter seeking solace. They came for different reasons: to help, to stay, to share a meal, or simply to see the faces of other women.

Rahila came up with the idea to start a small bazaar in the courtyard – a way to open their doors even further to the community. It would allow people to witness how much the prison had transformed, give the women an opportunity to earn a bit of money, and, most importantly, offer a step toward their independence.

Since the first market, their popularity only continued to grow. The governor herself attended the last one, and after their small community was featured in the papers, more and more women found their way to their door.

Some women stayed only briefly, using the refuge as a place to establish their next step. Others came simply seeking support, to find a sense of community when everything else felt lost. For many, it was a space to be reminded that the world had opportunities for them now, too. A small job board was added near the entrance, featuring new openings across the city, from tailoring shops to schools in need of teachers. Most women, after meeting with a doctor, social worker, or counselor from the local university, would leave with renewed confidence and a clearer path forward.

After the governor had made her rounds, purchasing small trinkets and chatting with the women, she pulled Zarmina aside. Shahar had followed the two of them up into their newly refurbished office space, offering Roya chai tea and kulcha.

"You should be proud of the work you've done here," she remarked in between sips of her tea.

"We are very proud." Zarmina looked to Shahar in that moment, a smile shared between them. It had only been two months at that point since the men had disappeared. They had made progress that would've maybe taken years, if ever, had this blessing not been granted.

"The way things are going, it won't be long until you are beyond capacity again." Zarmina thought of the reporters who had arrived with the governor. As word spread, more and more women would find their way to their doors.

"The job boards have been very helpful. The women are eager to get back to work."

Since the first official visit, one of the governor's representatives, Farzana had stopped by the refuge weekly to check on the women, delivering provisions such as food, clothing, cleaning supplies, and fresh bedding. Each time she would visit, Shahar would give her a list and whether it was hygiene products, books, or materials to repair the building, she always made sure the supplies arrived.

It was during one of her visits that Farzana casually mentioned the city's need for workers as government buildings, factories and farms began to reopen. The comment sparked an idea for Shahar to create a job board for the women, giving the women who felt trapped there a chance to grow again.

Within days, the board was up, covered with job listings ranging from farming and factory work to teaching and office jobs.

Now, the board is updated several times a week as new opportunities pour in. Women gather around it, scanning for roles that match their skills or interests. For many, it's their first time earning their own money. The sense of pride and independence is palpable, and each job taken is another small victory, another step toward rebuilding their lives and reshaping their futures.

"The men's prison is empty now, you know?" Roya said, pulling Zarmina from her thoughts.

"Yes."

Zarmina had read about it in the papers the week before. The decision to reintegrate the remaining male prisoners into the workforce had made headlines. Most of the men still imprisoned had been there for dissent-related crimes, while others were serving time for petty theft or drug trafficking. But with the city's urgent need for laborers, and the nature of their crimes, the authorities deemed it necessary to set them free.

"We have no plans for the building as of now. It is very large. You could do a lot with a space like that."

At Zarmina's silence, Roya set her tea down and stood, sending them both a small smile and nod as she went to leave.

"Think about it."

Shortly after Roya's visit, Farzana came to take Zarmina, Shahar, and a few of the other women on the short walk to the men's prison. The gates stood wide open, revealing an abandoned behemoth, its dark history etched into every surface. The place seemed haunted, as if ghosts lingered in every shadow, filling the vast, empty halls with an eerie silence.

But despite the oppressive atmosphere, the sheer size of it was impossible to ignore – it was easily fifty times larger than the women's prison.

The entire women's facility could fit comfortably within the yard alone, a barren expanse of land that Zarmina immediately envisioned transforming into a lush garden or orchard. She imagined rows of apricot trees swaying in the breeze, women harvesting and drying the fruit under the sun, the empty brown space blossoming with purpose.

There was room to grow, to breathe, to live. Every building was a new opportunity for religious courses, job training, therapy even. A concept foreign to many of these women.

As they moved through the haunted corridors, Zarmina's mind raced with possibilities. Passing each cell, she tried to picture a future where the heavy iron doors were gone, replaced with colorful tapestries or beaded curtains that swayed gently in the wind. It would still bear the marks of a prison, its windows small and barred, but with time, they could create something far greater than what it had been.

If they took over the male prison, they could dream so much bigger. Maybe even open their doors to women from other countries who experienced similar oppression, a sanctuary for any woman seeking safety and a fresh start.

"Look at what we've done to this place. It's come so far from what we knew for so many years." It was as if Shahar had known the exact direction Zarmina's mind had taken.

Zarmina had already decided they would accept the Governor's offer to move into the men's prison. Today was to be their last bazaar in the small courtyard of the women's prison.

Zarmina watches as a few women below turn toward the heavy doors set between the unguarded tall gates. As the door creaks open, two women in long black burqas hesitantly step inside, their heads bowed, movements cautious.

Zarmina feels the urge to rush down to them – to embrace them, to offer reassurance – but something holds her back. Instead, she lingers at the office window, watching the courtyard below. At the entrance, a few women step forward to guide them inside, greeting the newcomers with low voices and soft smiles.

One of the girls they are talking to is Rahila, a scarf loose around her neck, her long hair braided and twisted to the side. Zarmina can't hear what they're saying, but Rahila's arms rest gently on one woman's shoulder, heads bent together almost conspiratorially. After a moment, the one turns to the other for a brief moment before Rahila nods and steps back with a wide smile.

"It wouldn't take long to do the same at the men's prison. To make it wholly ours as we have done with this space."

Zarmina turns at Shahar's voice as one of the newcomers below reaches back behind her head, the black mesh slipping down to reveal her hesitant smile.

Zarmina finds the smile from the woman's lips pulling at her own, turning to find it mirrored on Shahar's own face.

"No. No, it wouldn't"

Day Ninety-Six: Nari – Cambridge, United Kingdom

So why was it only men? I mean, If we are sticking with the theory –"

"Oh, come off it! You know it's a lot more than a theory at this point," Natalia cuts in, her arms crossed, eyebrows raised in challenge.

Thomas ignores her, talking over her outburst. "If we are sticking with this *theory* then why did only men disappear? You know there have been female sexual abusers too."

A few of the women in the room groan, others sigh, and a wave of eye rolls ripple through the group. Nari watches with amusement, appreciating how smoothly everyone slips into their roles in this little ritual they all now take part in. The men, though few, seem to enjoy themselves just as much as the women, fully aware of the part they're expected to play. Once they cross the threshold into this room, no topic is off-limits, filters disappear, and no hard feelings follow anyone outside.

"Yeah, ok name one," Mercy challenges with an easy smile.

"Oh!" Luka pipes up excitedly. "That…uh schoolteacher who got pregnant from her student! They made a film about her." He snaps his fingers, looking to the group imploringly.

"Notes on a Scandal?" Piper questions with furrowed brows from beside him on the large loveseat.

"Yes! The kid was like twelve when it happened, and this lady teacher was in her thirties."

"Ok well, she wasn't, like, a predator out prowlin' the streets for male victims though. She was just fierce messed in the head," a familiar, lilting voice offers. Rory, a pretty redhead from Cork sits in a high back, swivel office chair behind the couch, her arms crossed at her chest, feet planted on the ground rocking her slightly from side to side.

"Uhh, well what about that one woman in America from the nineties." Thomas looks to the group, mirroring Luka's energy like they're team members on trivia night at the local pub.

"Aileen Wuornos!" Luka exclaims with excitement, jostling Piper beside him again.

"Yes! Like Aileen –," Thomas starts but is quickly cut off again by Rory.

"She wasn't a sexual predator you *berk*, she killed them because they were!" Rory snaps, though with no heat.

"Oi!" The exaggerated pout on his face clearly performative.

Natalia laughs, "Ok how about for fun, let's see if we can name famous male deviants." Now the few men in the room get a turn at rolling their eyes and crossing their arms in defeat as the women in the group erupt.

"Ted Bundy!"

"Jack the Ripper!"

"Edmund Kemper!"

"Oh, the Yorkshire Ripper!"

"The Scarborough Rapist -"

"Yes!" Thomas sits up from his slouch, bumping Nari beside him, like he's won the argument. "Wasn't that a brother and sister duo though? There you go!"

"No, I believe it was actually his wife who helped him." Nari says, smiling at Thomas' antics, trying her best to shimmy away on the overstuffed couch, Mercy huffing a small laugh from where she's pressed tightly against Nari's other side. Nari can admit one of her first truly western obsessions was true crime podcasts.

Nari used to love listening to the two women at night, their easy flowing conversation helping her sharpen her use of the English language. Korea didn't have many serial killers, not at the same volume the western world did. It was interesting how they'd glorify these horrifying stories and repeat them with so much sass. *Stay Sexy, Don't Get Murdered.* Why did so many women listen to true crime podcasts? It's like being a doomsday prepper, but the apocalypse is just everyday life.

"Exactly!" Thomas insists, as if she's only proven his point further.

Murmuring fills the sunlit room, the wind from the open, ivy-lined window carrying a cool, sweet breeze that cuts through the cramped, overheated space.

A slight creak calls the group's attention to the door, and they all turn in their various seats as Professor Bratton's face appears in the doorway, a tennis bag slung over his shoulder.

"Sorry to interrupt!" he chirps cheerfully, one hand held up in supplication, though the whole group responds with friendly greetings, as if they weren't just in the throes of an argument. "I'm taking off now. Just wanted to make sure you locked up when you left if I don't make it back in time."

Natalia shifts upright from where she's nestled in the cushioned window seat, sunlight filtering through the glass and pooling around her. A set of keys dangles from her fingers, catching the light as she flashes a reassuring smile. "Cheers!"

Natalia's family had immigrated to the UK from Russia during the collapse of the Soviet Union when she was only a few years old.

Now, in her late thirties, she was a postdoctoral researcher at Cambridge, focusing on gender and social inequality – a field which was now facing entirely new dimensions.

Natalia's mentor, Professor Bratton, had graciously offered up his home when she'd told him her idea for a small and casual discussion group that talked about the disappearances. The changes that had occurred in such a short amount of time were astounding, and she wanted to capture every angle of it while it was still fresh. She knew that these conversations, these thoughts, would be an important part of the historical narrative, helping people understand the old world as the new one grew all around them.

So instead of a cold classroom, or cramped library discussion room, the group met weekly in Professor Bratton's cozy home office for a few hours, tucked tightly together on the chairs and couches just like the books that lined the shelves of the room.

Natalia let the conversation flow and meander, no structure or direction. It was a safe space to confront their new reality. She recorded each one, transcribing the notes later to review with Professor Bratton, with the hopes that one day they could create a new class that explored these events - The Missing Men: Gender, Power, and Society Reimagined, she called it.

"Carry on! Oh, and don't forget to take some of Patrica's biscuits on the way out – candied orange peel this time!" He pats his stomach with a departing smile, shutting the door behind him as he leaves.

"Yeah, his wife was involved in at least three of the rapes and murders, including her own sister." Nari offers the disgusting truth into the brief silence that accompanies the snick of the door closing, wiping away the lingering thoughts of Mrs. Bratton's biscuits.

Mercy cuts in as Thomas opens his mouth to respond. "Sexual deviancy in women is merely a reaction to the actions of men." Thomas's mouth shuts with a quiet snap, the room quieting as her words settle in their minds.

"What do you mean by that?" Sebastian questions in a curious tone, normally one of the quieter ones in the group, a baby-faced Brit from Surrey.

"Well, take Aileen Wuornos," Mercy starts, the group now focused solely on her. Nari notes the small smile on Natalia's lips as Mercy begins.

"Her story starts long before Aileen took her first life, long before she became *Monster*. Do you know much about her childhood?"

"Yeah, I mean, I remember hearing she had a pretty rough go at it." Sebastian offers after another brief moment of silence.

"Aileen never met her father. He was put in prison for kidnapping and raping a seven-year-old child." Many of the people in the group grimace, but Mercy continues, unflinching in her words. "Her mother abandoned her and her brother, leaving them with their alcoholic grandparents. During that time, it's said she was continually abused by her grandfather. By the age of eleven, she was performing sex acts for cigarettes and alcohol." Sebastian's eyes are wide, his normally flushed cheeks pale.

"At fourteen she became pregnant, raped by a family friend, and by fifteen was homeless and forced to become a prostitute.

"By her thirties, when she committed her first murder, she had already been arrested over a dozen times and tried to kill herself numerous times as well. She had been destroyed by the world and men before she ever even had a chance."

The group sits in silence. A bird chirps from the tree outside. A car horn honks in the distance.

"You look back at any woman who has committed harmful sex acts against men, *or women*, there is history of violence in their own lives," Mercy concludes.

"So, you're saying essentially men are the root of all evil?" Luka questions.

"Well, ain't that how the saying goes?" Rory says with a playful smile.

Natalia laughs, "I think it's - money is the root of all evil."

"Even better – men with money are the root of all evil," Piper laughs.

"So, what about us then?" Sebastian asks, worrying at his lip as if this conversation will somehow decide his fate. "Do you really think all men are evil?"

"Of course that's not what she's saying," Piper says, reaching across Luka to tousle Sebastian's hair where he sits on an overstuffed leather ottoman.

"No," Mercy agrees. "Of course not. I mean plenty of men passed the test. You still being here proves it." Luka barks out an incredulous laugh at the playfulness in Mercy's tone, but Nari notes the contemplative look on Sebastian's face, the slight dip in his brows.

The now infamous article sparked intense debate. Many critics argued that the authors had oversimplified the complexities of the issue, leaving more questions than answers. While some of the disappeared had a history of clear violence, others had none, fueling speculation that the data was incorrect, while others speculated that perhaps their darker tendencies may have simply been dormant, waiting to surface. Perhaps they were the ones lurking on the fringes of society, visiting dark web forums and indulging in the vicarious thrill of others' misdeeds – acts they hadn't yet summoned the nerve to commit themselves. And then there were the manipulators, so skilled at controlling others that even their victims hadn't yet realized they were being abused.

Nari had been one of those women, Edward's sleight of hand so cunning it had taken such a brutal wake-up call for her to even examine the possibility of its truth. For weeks, Nari mourned the loss of Edward, and every little inane detail of their future she had spent her days fantasizing about. She had never once paused to examine his darker side, the small glimpses she'd witness from time to time and the questions that followed, all those little moments she had buried down so deep. If you repeated to yourself enough times that something was meaningless, you might eventually start to believe it.

It took her even longer to recover from the realization once the spell had broken; to pull herself out of the spiral of self-hatred that tore her up from the inside. Nari had come to Cambridge with this grand idea of becoming independent, of forging her own path in the world and growing into a different kind of woman than her mother. Her mother, who had spent decades folding herself into the mold of Korean expectations – always gracious, always accommodating, never raising her voice – had seemed to Nari like the epitome of submission. But instead of breaking away, she had fallen prey to a charming smile and practiced deceit, clinging to a man who promised her the world but expected everything in return.

After that, the dreams of Edward twisted into darkness, dark memories flooding back unbidden and replaying on repeat behind her eyes. How had she not seen it earlier? Had she simply refused to see? The moments when she had remembered trying to say no, drinks and sweet words molding her into complacency. The mornings she would wake up sore and hungover, but then he'd appear, his loving eyes and smiling face, a breakfast sandwich and matcha latte from her favorite local spot. The way he'd tell her he loved her, how he looked into her eyes so adoringly.

The realization had made her feel weak and pathetic, like she'd failed not just herself but the ideal she had been chasing. Worse, it brought with it the aching understanding that in trying so hard to reject her mother's choices, she had completely misunderstood them.

Her mother's happiness, her contentment, wasn't a prison, as Nari had once imagined it, but a choice. In failing to see that, Nari had missed the opportunity to understand her mother on a deeper level, instead projecting her own frustrations onto a woman who, perhaps, was far more independent than she'd ever given her credit for.

Nari was beginning to understand that a part of being a true feminist was respecting how other women chose to live their lives, even if those choices didn't align with her own vision of independence.

Mercy pulled her through it, and slowly Nari filled in the hole that Edward had left in his wake. In her darkest hours though, Nari would wonder what might've happened if Edward had never been taken away. Would she have realized eventually? How many years of his disguised abuse would she have accepted before she reached her breaking point?

Two weeks after the article was published, Nari discovered three new comments on Edward's page, each one more damning than the last. By the end of that week, the engagement ring had been mailed safely back to Edward's mother via an address his brother had given her, and Nari was boarding a plane back to Korea. Nari arrived back in Cambridge just as classes resumed, closer with her mother than ever before.

"You really believe that?" Sebastian asks. "That it was God or something who took them all?"

"I think, based on the men's particular common affinity, it was most likely Lucifer himself who came to collect them all," Rory laughs even as Sebastian slightly pales.

During their last meeting, the group had gone around the room and talked briefly about people they knew who disappeared, Natalia making it very clear that nobody had to share any more than they were comfortable with. Sebastian had shown surprising bravery that day and told the class that as a child he was abused by his pastor. That his mother hadn't believed him and for years he had grappled with the weight of that guilt, anger and shame. Finding out that the pastor had disappeared and then seeing the article announcing to the world his sins had been a vindication that Sebastian didn't know he'd been waiting for. He'd had a difficult relationship with God, but the idea that the world had been cleansed of them all was helping him find his way back.

"Maybe God has been a woman all along and she was just sick of men getting away with it," Rory says with a satisfied grin, and Nari is relieved to find Sebastian smiling softly in return.

"It's not like men always got away with it though," Thomas says.

"No, you're right. But the stats showed that out of the disappeared, only 78% had convictions, but that's still another… ," Natalia looks to be doing math in her head for a moment before huffing out, "millions who got away with crimes."

"Society has always had a way of protecting men," Nari says softly, more to herself than the others. In doing her own research, Nari had uncovered evidence that Edward's behavior had started years before they had ever met. Whispers of out-of-court settlements, cash payments from the family vault. It painted a picture of a man who had refined his craft over the years, his bad behavior only becoming better disguised.

"What do you mean?" Sebastian asks earnestly.

"Well, I mean, when there's a case in the news, we always look first at the women," Nari begins, looking around the group.

"It's as if our first instinct is to try and find cracks in her story instead of easily believing the truth of it. As a society it's like we rally behind the offender, especially if they are rich and famous. People go online and say things like – 'oh she's too ugly for him', or 'she's just looking for attention or money.' But these women get horribly destroyed online. A stack of cash can't buy them peace or a new life. When a girl gets raped at a college party it's always – 'what was she wearing? how much was she drinking? was she flirting with the boy or dancing suggestively?' Who cares? He could be half inside of her, and she still has the right to say 'oh, never mind' and he has to stop. And if she doesn't have the ability to say 'yes' or 'no,' then the answer is always 'no.'" Nari feels her cheeks flush under the weight of the collective attention. Sebastian's honesty those months ago had inspired her to share a piece of her own, recounting a brief, careful explanation of her relationship with Edward and his disappearance.

Now, as the room sits in silence, she can't help but wonder if any of them aren't contemplating her words, but instead replaying her earlier confession in their minds, finding the threads between what she's saying now and her past experience.

Mercy, sensing her discomfort, presses in a little closer on the already stuffed couch as she fills the gaping silence. "Society isn't the only thing that's always protecting men. Religion has been justifying violence against women since the beginning of time."

"Go on, then," Natalia says, sitting up in the window, her legs tucked into her chest, eyes bright with interest.

"Look at Eve. A woman who just wanted to be more than Adam's companion, painted as being responsible for humanities 'fall from grace.' Her thirst for knowledge led to endless narratives that paint women as inherently sinful, weak creatures full of deceit. Take Lilith, a woman who was literally demonized for refusing to submit to the same, probably super fucking boring man."

A few of the group laugh but Mercy pushes on, "If anything, this has shown us that religion couldn't really protect these men after all. That it hadn't really been all along. Look at what's happened in Afghanistan."

"That whole regime practically vanished overnight," Thomas says in response, his more playful mood from earlier turned subdued.

"The women there are thriving, they really are. And the whole country with them. Mark my words, there'll be some incredible things coming out of that place in the next few years. Sure, when you've held women back for so long, it's only natural there'd be a kind of renaissance," Rory says with an almost awed expression.

"Same with Somalia, Chad, the DRC. Once ranked some of the worst places for women in the world," Mercy adds, her eyes bright. Nari and Mercy had talked at length about the changes that had been happening in Kenya and all throughout Africa. Mercy hadn't travelled her continent outside of Nairobi; she knew how dangerous some parts of her world were. But she had gone to the protests in her city, seen them happening in other countries. Long before the disappearances, the women around Africa were rising up, finding their voice, fighting against the oppressive patriarchy.

Now, there was no corner of the planet that hadn't been affected by these disappearances, but it had been especially drastic in countries where violence against women had become a social norm.

"At one point, if you looked at a list for the top ten worst countries for women, most of them were in Africa, with Afghanistan at number one. At least in many of our countries we still had our voice, but the violence against our women took on a more openly brutal form," Mercy says.

It had been reported at one point that ninety-nine percent of Somali girls had undergone female mutilation. Nari could never forget the night she and Mercy had spoken about it, about how lucky Mercy was to have the parents, the life that she did. To have seemingly escaped such a fate so narrowly, Somalia sharing its border with her own country.

"The ironic thing is that, on average, there were higher rates of violence against women in the Americas than in Africa," Natalia states, as the three men's eyebrows raise in surprise.

"It's funny how in America there was always this narrative about how safe and wonderful and free it was for women. The second we start to fight back against the government removing women's rights, you have men and women who would say, 'well, look how bad it is for women in Somalia, or Pakistan or Afghanistan.'

"Like, sure, women definitely seemed to have it worse elsewhere, but how does that ever justify the injustice? It's always, 'Oh, look how free our women are,' but then in the same breath, they shame us anytime one of us tries to live independently or authentically. We called other countries 'third world,' but if a woman in America didn't want to be a mother and instead focused on her career, suddenly she's a 'spinster.'

"Like Nari said, the women who come forward are harassed and shamed for it. Americans used to think they were so much better than everyone else but look at the man who was running for president! A man accused of rape and sexual misconduct by over twenty women – and still, over seventy million people, men and women, voted for him. And his running mate was up there talking about forcing women to have children! We weren't better, if anything, we were worse…" Piper finishes in a huff of frustrated breath. She is the only American in the group, and had been ranting at parties about how disgustingly backward America had become long before the men disappeared.

"Why do you think that is?" Luka asks. "Why did so many people vote for him when it was clear he was a piece of shite?"

"I don't know, honestly. Why do *you* think they did?" Piper challenges with a shrug, clear she's wondered the same things many times and come up short.

"I think people don't want to believe that evil can be so insidious. I think maybe it was denial for most of them?" Sebastian offers, clearly speaking from his own experience. How many times had people turned their eye, ignored their children just because the man accused was a leader in their church or community.

"Or maybe a way to justify their own behaviors?" Thomas suggests, looking contemplative.

"Well, it's not like every man who voted for him disappeared," Luka comments. "They clearly didn't all vote for him with bad intentions."

"You're right, but the outliers were few and far between," Piper reminds him. Over the months, the group who had published the sites with all the men's names, had continuously updated the statistics on those who disappeared. Adding a feature where people could view various interactive pie charts based on income, religion, race and political affiliation.

"What about the women who make false accusations? I know you were saying that coming out and accusing a man is a horrible experience for a woman, but there are those who do it when it's a lie anyway," Luka questions.

"Women don't go around casting accusation on men for no reason. Even in the rare case where someone did lie, there's always something behind it. And if it's not just one, but two, three, or even four women all saying the same thing? That fella's not innocent. Even if they were lying about the actual rape or assault – what did he do to them that made them want to ruin his life like that?" Rory arches a brow in a clear gesture of challenge.

Luka flashes her a smile and shrugs, relenting to the point.

In the end, it didn't matter. The truth had prevailed, and that was all that mattered. There had been a conversation one week, a hypothetical thrown out about whether more men would just disappear if they tried something with a woman. Would they simply vanish into thin air? Thankfully, no one had seemed to test that theory. The men in Cambridge were more cautious now, overly respectful of women they didn't know. It was a shift, a subtle but noticeable one, and Nari found herself quietly enjoying it. It was a strange kind of power, but it felt good.

"Did you hear about that girl in America who came forward and got the bloke she accused out of jail?" Thomas asks.

"Yeah, it was pretty messed up circumstances. It was actually the girl's father who abused her, who reported the crime and turned in all sorts of fake evidence. The cops hadn't even run DNA tests or confirmed the evidence. They just saw a white victim accusing a Black kid and called him guilty. He was a scared kid basically tricked into signing his future away," Nari says, thinking of the articles she'd seen only a month before. It had been big news, the public rallying around the girl's confession until the governor commuted his sentence and issued a pardon, effectively wiping his record clean.

The girl, Keira, hadn't even known what had happened. According to her story, she met Marcus at a party. He'd been sweet and respectful and hadn't done anything wrong. Her father, now among the disappeared, had been abusing her and her mother for years. When she came home late that night after the party, he was drunk and on a violent bender. He'd seen a notification from Marcus on her phone and exploded. Through the pain, she vaguely recalled him taking the pictures of the work he'd done on her, but like all of the memories of her father's abuse, she had kept them tucked tightly away.

She had forgotten the incident, her father had blocked Marcus online and she never dared reach out to him again, her trips with friends to late-night parties effectively halted. She never received the countless letters from Marcus's lawyer following the disappearances and wouldn't have known anything about the case if the lawyer hadn't tracked her down. Her father had gone on and pressed charges on her behalf, without her knowledge.

In the video clips accompanying the article, Marcus appeared happy, youthful, and vibrant, as though the years stolen from him by prison had been returned with his pardon. His mother stood beside him, tears streaming down her face, while his sister, who he thanked profusely, shyly lingered with a woman who appeared to be her partner in the background.

Nari remembers the video because she couldn't stop herself from staring at the two of them. His sister with her caramel-colored skin, her slight frame, dressed in a pair of loose overalls and a tube top under a long jacket, gold rimmed round glasses on her face, and long curly hair piled atop her head, her hand clutched by the woman beside her – tall, fair and frankly ethereal. It was one of Nari's defining, 'Am I not totally straight?' moments.

"And plus, we all know that it's such a low percentage of women who falsely accuse men. In America, for example, they say that false accusations of rape are like two to ten percent, though some studies have even suggested it's probably much lower. On the other side, the U.S. Department of Justice claimed that only about seventeen percent of men will be arrested for sex crimes at some point in their life. Over half of all the men in America disappeared! That is way more than seventeen percent. What does that tell you?" Piper questions.

"That there are far more unreported crimes than false accusations," Nari responds, thinking of her own circumstance, of all the others that have come to light over the past few months. So many women silenced, now finally free to speak their truths, the abusers no longer hiding in the shadows.

"I think the real proof is in the change we are seeing every day in the world. Unprecedented!" The group laughs, a word they've heard in nearly every news report for the past few months, but Natalia continues through the laughter, "But really, I mean, look at how much the world has changed in such a short amount of time."

"And it's not even in all the huge ways, you know, but it's the little things that get me now. Like, I fell asleep on the flight last month, sitting beside a random lad. Something I'd have never felt comfortable doing before," Rory says, continuing Natalia's line of thought.

"Really? Why?" Luka prompts, his face scrunched in confusion.

"I just don't like the idea of being asleep around a strange man in a confined dark space," she explains easily, his features relaxing as he turns her words over in her head.

"Makes sense," Sebastian admits.

"And simple things like going out for a drink and not worrying about someone following me home or slipping something in my cup," Mercy adds with a shrug.

"The vibe when you go out is completely different now. Back in my clubbin' days, I'd dress up all sexy with my mates, but the second I walked into a place, the attention from all the men would make my skin crawl. Now, I can head out in a slinky dress or even a pair of trackies, and it doesn't matter," Natalia says, relaxed where she sits in the window seat, one leg now draped over the side, the other pulled against her chest.

"The male gaze," Nari murmurs in agreement, the image of Edward's bright blue eyes finding her across a room flashing before her eyes.

"Yes! It always felt so predatory," Piper agrees.

"Even just walking alone, being able to listen to music full blast, not always looking over my shoulder every time I'm out in public at night. Having to double bolt my door, worried someone might break in in the middle of the night," Mercy continues, the men in the room watching her as the women nod in agreement.

"It's like the burden is no longer ours," Nari says, her eyes turning pointedly to the three men in the group.

"For so long, it was on us to protect ourselves from men's violent urges. Holding our car keys between our fingers in case we had to use one as a weapon, tasers disguised as lipstick tubes, pepper spray on keychains, hair clips that double as knives. It's ridiculous! But now it's your time. Your time to pick up the slack. To be part of a new wave of men who are different from the last."

"Yes," Piper agrees, picking up Nari's thread. "For years, we let men get away with it. We watched our sons pull girls' hair, lift up their skirts, and instead of teaching them it was wrong, we brushed it off with a dismissive 'boys will be boys,' as if that excused it. As if that made it acceptable. Boys were boys – and look what happened.

"We turned into a society that voted for politicians who treated women like property to be kept and bred. We turned a blind eye to pastors and religious leaders who destroyed boys' and girls' lives and stole their innocence and futures. We ignored the cries of women trafficked by billionaires into sex slavery, trapped in filthy, dark rooms, drugged to endure the unthinkable just to survive another day.

"And now, every man who ever thought that kind of behavior was okay – every man who excused it, enabled it, or turned it into a way to make money – is gone. The threat erased completely," Piper finishes with a familiar gleam in her eye. It's one Nari's seen many times recently. Women walking with their heads held high, their voices loud, opinions finally considered.

"But it's us too as women. Our responsibility to make sure our voices are always heard. That no matter what happens we will never be silenced again," Nari says into the building silence.

What they were building wasn't a world anyone could've dreamed of. Instead of a dystopian nightmare, it was a utopian dream – a future humanity never could've imagined. Because, after all, the world had been shaped by generations of men who had spent their whole lives being told, boys will be boys.

Afterword

When I first decided to write this book, I knew that it had to be through the eyes of a diverse group of women from all over the world, with different cultural and social backgrounds. Because despite all of our differences as women, there is still much that we experience that is the same.

I'm a white woman, and I know that I can never fully comprehend a woman's experience from a different race, religion, or culture. But people say to write what you know, and I know a lot about the female experience. I have always been captivated by women's unique stories, and what the world would look if men didn't work so hard to hold us back.

Zarmina was definitely the hardest character for me to write. She comes from a vastly different culture than I do, one that I haven't become as familiar with over the years. At the same time, I felt her character and story were so important to this book. Afghanistan has been war torn and under Taliban rule for years, the country ranked lowest in the Peace and Security Index for women. I knew that the absence of the Taliban and its followers would have a very different impact on the women of Afghanistan, compared to the women of North America and Western Europe. At the same time, I needed to be able to show that while many men disappear from Afghanistan, there are also a great deal that go missing from every other country as well. That oppression can be insidious and that it has many different faces.

I prepared for Zarmina's story by studying some of the history of Afghanistan – the civil war, the women, Islam, customs and clothing, but despite all the hours of reading, I'm fully aware of the fact that I still barely scratched the surface. I focused a great deal on blogs written by women who had lived there and was moved and inspired by their stories and experiences.

I hope that I did her story justice.

Here are a few of the resources I came across during my research that were helpful in shaping her story:
- https://www.vday.org/afghan-women-speak/
- https://www.minaslist.org/blog
- A Girl in the River: The Price of Forgiveness

Acknowledgements

I have to thank my sister first. Her support over the years has become an invaluable part of my life. She's read everything I've written, been there through every anxiety attack (which there have been many) and has also been there for some of the happiest and most exciting moments in my life. Without your support, I wouldn't have been able to finish this book or have found the words to do so.

To my husband, thank you for listening to me constantly ramble about made up people and situations.

To my friends and family who read my work, who beta'd, who gave me feedback. I love you!

Big thanks to Pam Glazier for offering me invaluable writing advice, and to Marsha Worlock for reading through my final draft and helping catch any errors I might've missed after endlessly combing through the pages until I couldn't see straight.

To Gisele Pelicot, whose story came out while I was still shaping these thoughts. Your strength is an inspiration to us all.

And to Terrie, Tayler, Karen, and Joan. The women I've lost in my life, each of whom played a huge part in shaping me into the woman I am today.

www.ingramcontent.com/pod-product-compliance
Lightning Source LLC
Chambersburg PA
CBHW020026310726
48970CB00007B/2205